Ways Beneath the Skies

Clays Beneath the Skies

M. C. A. Hogarth

Clays Beneath the Skies

Copyright 2011 by Stardancer Studios

All rights reserved. No part of this publication may be reproduced, stored in a retrieval system, or transmitted, in any form or by any means, electronic, mechanical, photocopying, or otherwise, without the prior written permission of the author. All characters and events portrayed herein are fictional, and any resemblance to real people or incidents is purely coincidental.

M. Hogarth
PMB 109
13176 North Dale Mabry Blvd
Tampa, FL 33618

EAN-13: 978-0615490892
ISBN-10: 0615490891

Designed and typeset by Catspaw DTP Services
http://www.catspawdtp.com/

First printing 2011

10 9 8 7 6 5 4 3 2 1

Table of Contents

Foreword . . . . *x*

Freedom, Spiced and Drunk 1

New Stories 21

A Trifold Spiral Knot. 35

Money for Sorrow, Made Joy 55

Unspeakable. 79

His Neuter Face. 107

Fire in the Void 151

Chronology *173*

Jokku Riha: a Short Glossary *175*

Patrons *181*

Illustrations

The Runaway . . . . *xii*

The Healer 18

The Knot. 34

The Horizon. 54

The Storyteller. 78

The City 106

The Diviner .150

Foreword

IT'S BEEN TEN YEARS since I first encountered Maggie Hogarth's Jokka, and I can still remember the pleasure of that first reading. Maggie's a talented writer whose stories evoke not just characters but entire worlds, and reading her short fiction always feels a little bit like swimming in an alien atmosphere.

The Jokka stories hold a particular fascination for me, though. One of the strengths of speculative fiction is that it allows writers to extend and expand ideas past the realm of human reality. While students of human behavior debate the extent to which our actions are shaped by our biology, Maggie Hogarth has created a non-human society in which biological determinism is an absolute reality. For the Jokka, the physical demands of reproduction take an extreme toll on both the body and the mind; the two reproductive genders face the inevitability of "mind-death", the effective loss of their higher brain functions.

Characters imagine wistfully the possibility of a father reading bedtime stories to his children, or a mother holding her own grandchildren—these small things that humans take for granted are barred to the Jokka because of their biological limits. This leaves the third gender, the neuters, to assume responsibility for the maintenance of society and clan.

By creating a society so tightly and inextricably bound to biology, Maggie has thrown a sharp light on the nature of restriction in any society, ours included. Every character in the Jokka stories is shaped by the restrictions their society (and their biology) impose upon them. The joy and the struggle in these stories derives from the character's attempts to either adapt to or resist that which they cannot change, and the true immutability of those restrictions creates an extra layer of emotional connection for the reader. I also find that it creates an additional sense of hope for me, as a reader. If Kediil and Tañel and Nashada can find a way to create their own paths through such a tightly constructed and rigidly controlled society, surely we can do at least as much in a world where we have so much more freedom.

And, in the end, maybe analyzing society and determinism is beside the point. Maybe it's best to take the Jokka stories just on their own internal merits—enjoy them for the rich storytelling and the vivid worldbuilding, for the love and the sorrow and the passions of the characters. Either way, it's a world well worth spending time in.

Susan Marie Groppi
Former editor of Strange Horizons

Freedom, Spiced and Drunk

BEFORE HER MIND DIED, my mother told me to speak all my memories into a conch shell before my clan gave me to a male. She showed me her own fragile talisman, let me rub my fingers along its slick white surface and smell its sea-salt fragrance. She said, be sure to examine it for holes other than its mouth, lest the words whispered into it leak away. If they do, the memories will be forever lost when pregnancy takes your mind.

I was female then, and the certainty in her stone-gray eyes had softened my fears of impending senility. No anadi, no female, can escape the mind-death. It may claim you while you carry your first child or wait until your sixth, but it will claim you. So we were taught, and so Nature ordains.

The conch did not restore my mother's memories after my second brother abandoned her body, wailing to Ke Bakil's bright sun. I mourned her as if she had died, in lieu of mourning for myself.

I was born anadi and beautiful, and so my clan anticipated my sale with great joy. Those born anadi usually remained thus.

The warm breath that carried praise blew soft across my scaled skin as my family examined me for flaws with each occurrence of the flame in the northern sky. How they adored my long mane of pale glitter and gold! How they loved to spread it over my shoulders and breasts and comment on how well it matched my body, painted by Nature with the iridescence of *sukul*, the color of a white shell beneath the light of a full moon. Kediil, they said to me, when the gods wove you, they used a warp of moon's rays and a weft of sun. You are spun light, with the sea in your eyes. When you go to your mate, you will enrich your family with several new anadi, and perhaps even another eperu.

For this, then, are all females born: to increase the family, in their bodies and their mate-prices.

My father noticed the first sign of my impending maturation, and the crease in his brow and his flattened ears marked his unease. "You've lost weight," he observed. "Have you been exerting yourself too much?"

"No, ke riiket," I said. *No, honored Father.*

One of my aunts, her mind only partially claimed even after three children, touched my cheek. "Your eyes are different."

And then puberty came, and with it the change my family had been praying to avert.

I was Turning neuter.

As the days waxed long and the fat sloughed from my hips and breasts, I escaped the camp for the solitude of the plains where I could dance in the scrub alone, unafraid at last of the heat or the fragrance of my sweat. The mind-death would not claim me now, not in pregnancy, not during the effort of my body, not in the grip of the sun and air. I would not be sold for my clan's wealth; instead, the first among eperu would train me to hunt and harvest, to herd and run and thrive.

I had no more need for conchs or spells. Nature had delivered me from useless talismans into freedom, to the spiced scent of Its grasses at ripest summer.

"You seem eager to stand apart."

I turned, faced the elegant figure of ke Mardin, first among the eperu, the neuters. The sun shone in Mardin's sand-hued skin and winked in the polished gems braided into its red mane, and the breeze brushed its tail and the grasses in one long stroke. Mardin was only another element of the world, the amber plains, the wind-torn clouds.

"This is living, ke eperu," I said, touching my breastbone in the neuters' greeting. "This is life. This place, this smell, this aloneness."

"Kediil, Kediil," the eperu said, shook its head once. "We should have known you would Turn. Your spirit lives in your heart, just like any eperu's."

I blushed white at the ears. This praise fell warmer and sweeter on my skin than any other, for I had never believed my spirit lived in my womb, as an anadi's did. "When may I start the learning, ke Mardin?"

"So hungry?" Its wry smile did not disguise the kindness in its eyes. "You know it is best to wait until the sky flame returns before assuming this Turning is your last."

"I will do as you think wise, ke eperu," I said, resting my eyes on the horizon. How novel distance is to those whose lives are spent hiding from work and light in tents!

Mardin stood beside me, shoulder to shoulder. It had been born eperu and stayed thus all its life, one of the few who had no trace of an emodo's thickness of sinew or an anadi's heavy frame. I longed for its lissome grace to be blown by the wind into my body.

"Jokku wisdom must sometimes give ground to the heart's desires," Mardin said. "Follow me and I will teach you the knowledge that can only be learned from a hard run."

Beside a pool in the shadow of the mountains, I dropped to my knees. Cupping my hands in the still waters, I trapped the essence of the clouds and brought it to my lips. Then I rolled onto my side, bruising the short grasses beneath my body, and napped beneath a wind that tickled my naked skin with floating seeds.

As the other eperu danced around a fire that kicked away the vespertine dark, my companion passed me a clay goblet of spirits. My fingers traced the sharp division between rough clay and slick glaze as I accepted, and the moon-cold bit my tongue through the sharp liquid as I swallowed. I clapped for the neuters whose shadows rarely touched their feet, so often and high they leaped.

With a basket balanced on my head, I reached for the brown fruits hanging from the smooth gray limbs of the nearest tree. Their pungent odor stung my nostrils, but I looked forward to the flavor of the oil the other eperu were pressing, closer to the camp.

The summer's heat had abated, but the world rarely grew

too cool during the day. Beads of sweat dropped from the arm that steadied the basket, which sat easily. My body had grown accustomed to frequent use; I had learned to inhabit it.

The sky flame returned, brilliant green and blue sheets quivering on the horizon. Mardin found me dancing in rapture by the horizon's eerie green light. It did not pause, but stepped into my circle and joined me in my celebration. Its hands strayed to my hips, and, warmed by our exertions, we fell to a different sort of pleasure.

Mardin propped itself on one of its elbows and looked down at me as I panted. "Enjoy?"

"I thought only breeders had that," I said, well pleased.

"We are all one," Mardin said. "Not so different from each other. Our bodies are all born with the same potentials. Why then can the eperu not keep this? We are best suited to enjoy it."

I thought of the dizziness I'd often felt after pleasure as an anadi. Other females had been known to faint. As eperu, I knew only an expansive peace, and the familiar, friendly ache of an exercised body. "And what other secrets have you been hiding from me, that I might now know as a true eperu?" I asked, teasing Mardin's chin with my fingertips. "Or are these secrets only known by you, wisest of the wise?"

"They are eperu secrets, truly," Mardin said. "But you have remained eperu throughout the cycle of the seasons, so they are yours now as well."

"And what are they?"

Mardin laughed. "As if I could tell it all to you now! And as if telling would be enough! You must partake of the secrets that are now yours to truly own them. They hide in plants."

"And what," I asked, still stroking Mardin's face, "will these mysterious plants whisper to me?"

"Each one has its own wisdom," Mardin answered. It nipped my finger, then took the tip into its mouth and sucked until it drew my claw. A moment later, it continued, "Some open you to Nature's embrace. Others slow the world, or quicken it. Some clear the mind, or defray the cost of too much dancing the previous night. Some are so potent they will stop your heart; others so gentle your mother's touch is harsher."

"All this power in plants?" I asked, breathless, for Mardin had a talented mouth. "Surely not."

"Taste and see. Eat and learn. The knowledge is yours now, to take, to keep," Mardin said, its arm running down my hip. Soon we both set aside any thought of plants at all.

The following morning I rolled onto my side with a groan and rubbed my eyes. There are still limits for the tireless eperu, and we'd found them. The finding had been pleasant, though, so who could complain?

Mardin's feet appeared beside my head. When I looked up, its head blocked the sun. "Good morning, sleepy."

"That's a strong-shining star," I said. "Wake me when the real sun rises."

"Silly eperu," Mardin said. "I am twice your age near enough, and *I* am on my feet. Lift your head and greet your lover. It has a gift for you."

I dragged myself upright and Mardin pressed a steaming cup into my hand. The rising moisture dampened my nose and brought to it the fragrance of spices and something bitter. I lapped once at its surface, then took a long drought. Bright energy flooded my body.

With a gasp, I looked up at Mardin. "The first of the secrets?"

It touched my lips, its eyes full. "Drink and learn."

In any Jokku clan, there is an eperu whose knowledge of the earth's drugs cannot be surpassed. In our clan, that master was Mardin. For the lore-knower to also be the first among eperu was unusual, but Mardin had only recently taken the position of first.

This suited me well. With the knower as my lover, I learned quickly. It was just as Mardin had said: there seemed to be a plant for everything.

Learning of plants was not my only new duty. As the sturdiest of the three sexes, the eperu were called upon for many labors. One of them was the birth watch, for though our hands were not as clever as an emodo's, we had the endurance to see an anadi through her pregnancy and to turn the baby if it had become twisted.

This skill, like every other, had to be learned through practice. Mardin took me to the birth tent to oversee the final hours of my aunt's pregnancy, the same aunt who had seen through her clouded eyes the change in my face.

"There. Slip your hand in. It should be simple."

I hesitantly pressed my greased fingers inside my aunt's body, took a breath, then pushed deeper. I gasped.

"What do you feel?" Mardin asked.

"Feet! Tiny feet!" Just like mine, with four tender toes and thumb, the claw on the latter not yet grown, precious miniatures.

"Not good," Mardin said. "You will have to turn your cousin if she is to have egress."

"Is it female?" I asked.

"I don't know," Mardin said, grinning. "Is it?"

I stretched my fingers deeper, ran them over the little body. The area between the legs was smooth. "Anadi or eperu," I said.

"We shall call your cousin female until she arrives and we can know for certain. Can you feel how the turn is to be made?"

I thought I could. I grasped the little tail and made my best effort. When I could spread my fingers over the tiny face, I pulled back. "I think it is done."

Only then did I hear my aunt's mewling, see the sweat covering her body, the sweat so deadly to the breeders. Horrified, I checked her face, but with her eyes closed I could not tell how she fared.

"Aunt?" I asked, but she was gone, deep into the needs of her own body.

"See, the baby comes," Mardin said to me.

And indeed she did, almost too quickly for me to catch her before she hit the ground. And female she was, my newest cousin, perfect in every way... save her sex. Mardin cleared her mouth of mucus and she let out a sputtering cry. I thought bitterly then of my brother who had delivered my mother into the slavery of the mind-free, and checked my aunt.

Blank eyes met mine. This birth had been the one. My aunt, who had fended off Nature so long, had at last been claimed.

"Mardin!" I said. "Isn't there something we can do about this? Some plant that will save the breeders? Look at her! She was a person half a day ago, and now . . . now all her intelligence has fled to that child."

"Kediil—"

"No! I will not be quiet," I said, knowing the look in its eyes. "Surely Nature is not so cruel. Surely there is a way! There must be something. . . ."

"Hush!" Mardin said, grabbing my arm with such force I jumped. Startled into silence, I watched as it cleaned my cousin in a basin and swaddled her in a cloth before handing her to my father, the Clan's head, waiting outside. Then it gently washed my aunt, who could no longer wash herself, and helped her to the arms of the anadi.

Only then did Mardin take me by the arm and march me outside, and it did not stop until we were well, well away from the glittering tents. It sat me beneath a gnarled gray tree and crouched in front of me.

"You must watch your mouth before the others, Kediil."

"What! Why?"

It sighed. "Because there are plants that safeguard the breeders from the mind-death, and their use is forbidden."

I stared at Mardin, mouth ajar.

It sat beside me then, our shoulders and hips touching. "That this knowledge has been passed on through the lore-knowers is a mystery to me, for it would seem less trouble, less heart's pain to simply forget it. We have been silent—we must be silent—for we cannot allow the breeders to know. But every lore-knower knows how to let an anadi keep her mind."

What Mardin said was such an abomination that I knew that something dire prevented the release of the information. The exchange of knowledge among eperu and from the eperu to the breeders was a sacred thing, for the emodo and anadi could lose their minds at any time, depriving them of the understanding they would need to live on. Only the eperu could be trusted to remember, and we did, and this was half of our function, our reason for existing . . . the other half being to do the work that would otherwise shorten the mind-span of the breeders.

I took several long breaths through my nose, observing that spring waned by the heat that tickled my throat. "Tell me," I said.

"The plants that give the anadi and the emodo their shield also take from them their ability to breed."

"They . . ."

"Sterilize them, yes," Mardin said. Its lopsided smile did not reach its eyes. "The plants save the anadi or emodo at the expense of their ability to have children. It seems to be an unavoidable side effect."

"Surely it would be worth it," I said.

"Worth it!" Mardin sighed and took my hand, the one that so lately had turned my cousin, still sticky. "What anadi wouldn't want to keep her mind forever, cousin? What emodo wouldn't prefer to hunt for his children's meals, knowing that the exercise won't hurt his ability to sing them lullabies that night? Every anadi and every emodo faces the risk of the mind's death at one time in their life or another, no matter how strong they are, how sturdy, what sex they were in puberties. But if all of them chose the safer way, who would have the children?"

"You say that the race would die," I said. I shivered.

"I say that the way we have chosen was chosen for a reason," Mardin said, squeezing my fingers.

I noticed then the drying layer of mucus on my forearm and stood abruptly. "I need to wash."

Mardin did not stop me. Perhaps it knew that I needed to bathe more than my arm. My spirit felt dirty.

Though I wished with desperation to avoid any contact with those I was forbidden to save, my fingers were slender and I found myself on many birth watches. In some, my aunt or cousin or sister survived to gaze with tenderness on her child, to whisper sweet words to the tiny hairless ears. On some heart-stopping watches, Nature caught the mind only to lose its grip, and after a few stuttering sounds the clarity would return to the anadi's eyes with a sharp overlay of fear. How I ached to see that fear!

And of course in some, in many, I saw Nature take some or all of the female's mind, leaving her only the comfort of her new infant.

Each of these incidents added a stone to my spirit. I felt as heavy as the earth.

The day I left the clan was a day in the deep summer, with the sky so hard and flat a blue that we knew it would storm by afternoon. Most of the eperu rested in camp, for traveling during those summer storms was ill-advised for any Jokkad, no matter the sex.

I dozed in the sunlight near the tent of stores, enjoying the warmth on my skin, just barely tasting the spiced fragrance of grass and the scents of my family through the intense heat. On these storm days, I liked to rest in the open until the first few drops struck my belly, reminding me that I was Jokku, not one with the soil. Such had been my plan that day when a dozen cries jerked me from my reverie.

"What is it?" I asked one of the eperu running past.

"Quick, come! Thasenet has fallen!"

My breath jumped in my mouth and I leaped to follow. Thasenet was a favorite in the clan, our jeweler; his hands and feet were dexterous even for an emodo, and his quick wit and gentle spirit won everyone's affection. When I arrived, I found him sprawled on the ground, mane and tail splayed. He looked as if he slept, but, hunched over him, both Mardin and my father looked dismayed.

The first time Thasenet twitched, I thought I mistook my sight. By the third, I knew what ailed him; his motions were the uncontrolled flopping of a mind that no longer knew its limbs.

"How?" I asked, despairing.

"He went out, looking for sand and clay," one of the other emodo said, his face stricken. "We think he ran too hard. Running from something."

"An eightclaws," Mardin said, pointing at the fallen emodo's back. I saw a shallow slice along the back of his thighs. "The fear and the run took him."

Nature surely crowed today. To take an emodo's mind is much harder than to take an anadi's. I stepped back.

"Kediil," Mardin said, for perhaps it saw my soul in my eyes.

"We could not have helped him."

But I knew it lied.

I turned, fumbling my first step, and almost fell. But then I was running, knowing it would never kill me, never steal my mind from me. Deep into the wilds I ran, away from Jokka, away from my clan, away from the tents where the eperu were forced to watch their family die, one by one.

The summer storm did eventually come. It found me far from home, curled up in a nook of rock near the bones of the old mountains.

I feared that the others would come for me. Each day I traveled further, until my foot touched ground in places too far for the other eperu to travel.

This freedom from civilization, from the pathos of my view of the camp, suited me well. I hunted my own food. Drank water from swift streams and still ponds. Slept in trees soft with leaves.

Brewed my own drugs, and sipped them to forget, or remember, depending on my desire at the time.

Climbing the slope of one of the gray mountains in fall, I tore my loin-skirt. Once I reached a plateau I could sit upon, I examined it and realized it was beyond saving. I untied it from my hips, ran my hands over its soiled surface. The cloth had frayed at the edges; the tassels had unraveled.

I cast it over the edge of the rock and watched it fall, fluttering, to the earth. Then I turned my back on it and continued my efforts.

That winter I sought the plains again, for the mountains were colder than I liked. I reacquainted myself with the bitter scent of grass stunted by the season, with the stiffness of its blades when I rolled on it. Still there was enough to eat, spread in caches I had buried, and I thrived in the silence of the plains. My own company satisfied me more than I had anticipated, and even the few animals that interrupted my solitude proved an unwanted distraction.

Winter had half-ended when I clawed open another of my buried treasures and found in it not just the dried meat I had left, but a small box of precious wood. Perplexed I drew it out and sniffed it, but the acrid scent of the salt had obscured any evidence of the Jokkad who had placed it there. I glanced at the area and found no footprints—nor had I really expected any, for the earth over the cache had grown its own layer of grass, undisturbed since late summer at least.

I opened the box, found in it a new midnight blue loin-skirt, a damask with entwined thorn vines in deep brown edged in silver. Little silver blossoms, petals stylized into three teardrops, had been embroidered over the weave. With this loin-skirt were twin silver chains, one with moonstone beads and another with hematite.

I ran my finger over the smooth stones, ignoring the itch that presaged tears. I knew who had left the box. Mardin would never directly ask me to return, but knowing that it missed me was enough. I folded the cloth and returned it to the box, the box to the cache, the soil to the hole. Then I ran again, tears dripping from my teeth.

The sky flame came at winter's end, marking the beginning of the new year. I noticed then the first sign: I wanted the fat off the grass-eater, not just the meat. My body waxed with the heat, and by spring's end I knew. My first puberty had not delivered me to my final sex. I was Turning again, much later than most Jokka. And as my people had only two possible puberties, this new sex would be the one I would live as all my remaining years.

When I discovered the swollen peaks on my chest, I sat on a rock and hugged my knees, hiding them from myself. Nature had decided to give me back my birth sex, ordinarily a sentence to a life of cloistered fear.

But now... now there was someone who could save me. And I had only a few weeks to find our camp again before summer came to stalk my thoughts with the spears of heat and sweat.

There wasn't time for wasting. I shook back my mane of glitter and gold and began my journey back.

Mindful of my increasing fragility, I traveled with deliberate care to the plains, stopping at the cache to pick up the box.

It wasn't there.

I rocked back on my pads, stunned. I hadn't realized how much Mardin's faith had meant to me until it had been withdrawn. With a shiver, I covered the hole again and stood. The eperu would help me. If not for what I was now, then in the name of what I had been. It had to.

A handful of days later, I stood beside a smooth tree within sight of the camp: tiny tents I could cover with my hand. I worried over how to approach them, for if I came too close, my father would usher me into a tent to keep me safe until he could sell me into another clan. As anadi, I belonged to my family, and my fate was not my own. I was not eager to hear their praise over my shimmering mane or moon-shell skin, nor to know just how many anadi and eperu I would fetch with my mate-price.

I slept during the worst heat of the day, aware of my shortness of breath, frightened by it. I worried I would not reach Mardin in time. I dreamed that I would die, but my body would not cease to move.

I woke to a delicious coolness, and found it was the shadow cast on me by the first among eperu. I climbed to my feet, let Mardin's eyes travel down me. I knew what it saw: that my breasts had become heavy, my hips broader and softer. I had not lost my slender figure yet, but given time and inactivity, even that would go. I was, for now, an eperu with breasts and hips.

In defiance, I touched my hand to my chest in greeting, instead of to my belly.

Mardin cast its head down, uttered an obscenity. My ears flicked back in surprise, for I'd never heard it curse before.

"Mardin," I said, then stepped toward it. "Mardin, help me."

It stared at me with wide eyes, then shuddered. "No."

"Please, Mardin," I said. "You know the ways. Help me keep my mind."

"Your father would kill me."

"I don't have to go back!"

A sudden silence, and the wind blew between us. It did not pick up the eperu's red mane. The sun did not play on its sand-hued skin. This time it was Mardin who seemed alienated from the world, not me.

"No one ever need know," I said. "You can tell me the secrets. I will partake and be safe, and the clan will still count me lost."

"But where will you go?" Mardin asked.

"Wherever the world takes me," I said.

Mardin's head fell. "But then I would never see you again."

I took another step toward it. "You could come with me!"

"No."

And I had known that answer before it had given it to me. Knew that it could no more abandon the camp than I could stay . . . for Mardin had become first among eperu for good cause, and it counted the anadi and emodo of my family its responsibility.

"Please, Mardin," I said again.

"You would have me give you the plants. You would sterilize yourself and run into the wild, where neither the clan nor I could have the benefit of your presence. All so you could keep your thoughts."

I shivered, horrified by the lack of tone in a voice I'd always found so rich. Yet I held up my head. "Not just my thoughts. My life. Yes, this would be my choice . . . though there are parts of it I would regret."

When Mardin lifted its head, its wry smile brought an itch to my teeth. My breath caught in my mouth. "Ah, Kediil. Truly your spirit lives in your heart."

It took my hand.

I woke late that night to find Mardin gone. The fire that had died unnoticed during our pleasures had been rebuilt. On it was a warming pot; beside it, the midnight blue loin-skirt and the hip chains.

I dressed and sat before the fire, waiting for the waxflower tea to steep. Then from the clay cup the eperu had left, I drank, my claws trailing along the glaze on the sides, and tasted a sharp liquid with a sun-hot bite. I thought of the life spreading before me . . . free to travel the broad back of the world, to meet other Jokka, to do with my life whatever seemed most appropriate. Tomorrow would be time enough to begin this joy.

Tonight . . . tonight I would dance in the scrub alone.

New Stories

SEDIKIT WAS DYING. I could smell the sharp tang of it on his breath, hear it in the strained hiss that passed between his parched and parted lips. I wrung the rag, letting the drip of the water displace for just a moment the sound of the male's distress. This sickness had already killed Marne's baby, the one that had stolen the last of her wit with its birth. In that, it claimed two victims, for I sorely missed Marne's humor.

Daridil stepped into the room, his passage ruffling the woven grass curtain hung in the door and allowing in the mingled scents of sun-baked clay and rikka sweat. I did not look at him, knowing what he would say.

"Deciding to stay was a mistake."

I sighed. The sun had seen this argument before, and no doubt would rise and fall many more times over it yet. "We have passed over this place dozens of times in our travels, Daridil. You know as well as I do that this is an unusually dry summer. It will go, as seasons do, and the rains will come."

"The rains were one thing. But this . . . don't you think it's a sign, Serel? How many more will we lose for breaking our customs?"

by M.C.A. Hogarth

I did look at him then, for his voice had a breathy flutter better suited to fear than his usual belligerence. Daridil was atypical for our kind: he'd remained male through both puberties, and it showed in the adult. Tall and limber, he had the emodo's long fingers and flexible toes, perfect for complex and delicate work. His wedge-shaped head had a handsomely blunt end that complemented the triangular ears with their dark tufts. He was in some ways too perfect, for the family tended to overlook his mind while praising his body.

"I don't think the sickness is related to our decision to stay here, truly," I said to him. "It is coincidence."

His narrowed eyes told me he didn't believe. He glanced at Sedikit and tossed his braided mane over his shoulder. "Well, I shall go burn incense for him. The Trifold is displeased with us."

"Gods are not cruel," I said.

"No. But errant children may mistake a cuffing for cruelty if they don't know better."

I sighed. "Daridil—"

"Pray we'll have no more cases of this," Daridil interrupted me. "Or we will abandon these ill-thought buildings." He lifted his chin and ducked back out.

The rustle of rushes brought my eyes back to Sedikit. I finished wringing out the rag and placed it over his forehead, flinching at the heat rising off his skin. We were not meant for heat, we Jokka. Too hot and our minds burn up and die, and the first to go are our breeders. I clasped one of the emodo's warm hands in my own, my fingers cooled by the water, and murmured, "I will not let you die."

Not only because I loved him, as I loved all our family. But because I would not release the two brick houses we'd spent so much effort erecting. Our new life—a life free of the constant indignities and hardships of travel—must prevail.

"There is a madwoman in the hills," Resa told me. It was glaring at the herbs it was attempting to grind into paste for the evening meal. I stood beside the youth, my shadow stretching outward in crisp violet on the dun ground. There were no clouds in the hard sky, and the heat rose from the earth in dense waves. No wonder there were no females or males outside the house.

"What rumor is this?" I said, crouching beside the eperu child.

"It's not a rumor," Resa said stubbornly. It stretched its fingers without releasing the pestle, then resumed its efforts, muscles tensing beneath its side and shoulder. "We went looking for vegetables. We found a doused campfire and then we saw her." It licked its lip. "Her fire smelled like medicine."

My ears twitched. "Are you sure?"

"Do I look nose-blind to you?" Resa asked, scowling. "It smelled like that liquid you have to drink when you're feverish. High, thin and bitter."

"A madwoman in the hills with a medicine-scented fire," I said aloud, affecting a nonchalance that had no relationship with my pounding heart. Could it be a lore knower? Would I be so lucky! "A strange tale."

"It's not a tale," Resa said. "Look for yourself." It pointed to the northwest. "Those hills."

"I suppose I will," I said. "Thanks, ba eperu."

Resa only sniffed and continued its labors.

I resisted the urge to check on Sedikit again and strode past the rikka tethered at our outermost building and into the northwestern hills. The land we had chosen for our settlement was beautiful when the sun wasn't baking it to char. We were near a deep pool and a stand of scattered trees, close enough to sit under their leaves but far enough to take advantage of other passing families on the main thoroughfare south. It wasn't a new idea, putting down roots: several other tribes had done so. They had chosen that course because of infirm members, or to remain near someone they'd buried. We had chosen it because I had convinced Daridil that there was some value in remaining in place. Because I was convinced that the constant travel shortened the lives of all our family, and our anadi, our females, especially. The anadi had the most fragile constitutions of all our sexes . . . even the burden of pregnancy often consumed their minds. So the concept of an anadi in the hills seemed outlandish. Females did not walk alone—

The point of a spear nudged my back and I halted.

"Mean me no harm and I will treat you the same," said a trembling but determined voice.

"I bear you no ill will," I said.

The pressure at my lower spine eased. I looked over my shoulder and found Resa's mysterious anadi there, looking like no anadi I'd ever seen. She was thin with barely any breast, and wore clothing without showing signs of discomfort at the heat. I could not decide whether to think of her as anadi—soft, frail and feminine—or eperu like myself, a hunter, a neuter, a hardened creature suited to the climate.

Something in my expression softened hers. She chuckled. "Am I confusing you?"

"I admit I didn't believe when I heard there was a female in the hills," I said. "You don't look like any female I've seen."

"That's because all the females you've seen have been pampered breeders. I am a fighter."

"Born eperu?" I asked. It was impolite to ask of a stranger, but curiosity had me in its teeth.

"Born anadi," she said. "Turned eperu at first puberty, then back female at second."

Perhaps it explained her endurance and her physique, though I'd known plenty of anadi who had been eperu and none of them looked like this creature. Most of us Turned; our first puberty was more likely to see us from one sex to another than our second, but the second still held potential. Why we were all given these experiences of another sex, why sometimes we blended the best, or worst, of their attributes into our final form, no one knew . . . but I felt for the stranger. I had been eperu, then emodo, and eperu again; never the weakest sex. "I see," I said. Then blushed pale at the ears. "I apologize for my curiosity. It's a weakness. I'm Serel of family Nudet."

"It is no trouble, Serel . . . for I'll have some questions from you, if you're done. I'm Kediil. What are you doing down there? Are you actually planning to stay in those houses all year?"

"Gods willing," I said.

Kediil shook her head in amazement. She had truly marvelous

skin . . . *sukul* we call it, moon-shell white. Her hair had been messily braided into an eperu style, but its color, a luminous silver-gilt over white, made the mess seem affected, beautiful. Even the smudges of brown soil and the pallor of a few bruises and scratches did not mar her appearance much.

"I have never heard of such a thing," she said. "Why?"

"Because the travel is hard on the breeders," I said.

"Ah," Kediil nodded. "Of course." And then we stared at one another, hers a look of great amusement and mine the embarrassed pause of someone who has realized the incongruity of its observation.

"Ah!" Kediil laughed. "I'm done teasing you with your preconceptions. Come sit by my fire and have something to drink. It's been long days since I've had company."

I followed her over the next rise, where she'd set up a small camp beneath a single, drooping tree. The anadi patted its trunk as she passed it, then dropped beside her fire and gently poked it back to life with a stick. The ceramic pot over it did indeed smell of heat-calming medicine; she did not pour from it, but from a smaller pot. I accepted the petal-tinted water.

"You know some of the way of plants?" I asked, sitting across from her and attempting to be casual.

"I know all of the way of plants," she said, glancing at me. "All that a lore knower should, at least."

So she had been taught by the lore knower of her family, a teaching traditionally given only to other neuters. "They thought you would stay eperu?"

Her ears flattened, but she gave the single dip of assent with her chin.

"My sorrow, Kediil."

"Why?" she asked with a flick of her tail. She grinned. "I am living a life I enjoy."

I rested my hands on my knees. "Do you offer your services to those in need?" When she looked up at me with lifted brow, I said, "I will not overlook aid whatever shape it comes in."

"Then you must truly have need," she said. "What's wrong?"

I took a deep breath. "There is a fever in the family. It has taken one of the babies, and now has settled on a male. His breath is sharp and comes hard to him. I think he'll die soon."

Kediil frowned. "There are many sicknesses with similar symptoms. I would have to see him."

I paused then, realized exactly what I did. Jokka do not travel alone. Breeders do not wander without family. This anadi could be mad, or have done wrong to be cast out . . . and bringing her home would win me no favor from Daridil. Particularly since we had no lore knower, a lack he never ceased to remind me of. It would have been my task, had Ikeser not died beneath the claws of an eightclaws before it could teach me.

"You're worried that bringing me to your home would be a poor idea," she guessed into my silence.

I blushed again, but met her eyes. "Yes."

"It would be," she said. "I have been in and out of the tents of the Jokka these many days I have been free. I have learned more than any lore knower I've met, for I've collected the wisdom of all those I've met in passing. Yet no Jokkad will come close to me. They fear that their anadi will take my madness and follow me into the wild." She laughed. "As if a life of hardship, of solitude is welcome to most!"

"And yet to you it is welcome," I said. "What are you to enjoy it?"

Kediil's head twisted, a gesture torn between sorrow and self-consciousness. She ran her finger over her toes, through the hair that grew to cover them. She'd clipped the ruffs very close. Said she, "I don't know, ke eperu."

I stood, brushed the dirt off my loin-skirts. "I will take you back with me, if you care to come, ke Kediil."

She looked up at me and smiled, faintly. "Where there is suffering, I care to heal."

The heat had driven the entire family to shelter; their fear of sickness into the house that had not seen the death of Marne's baby, nor now witnessed the decline of Sedikit. I led Kediil inside, watched her as she studied the walls and the door with its curtain. The building had only one room, and this one was smaller than the other where the family huddled. We were only a twice-handful: three males, three females, one neuter and three children . . . the travel had not been kind to us. And why do the Jokka roam? "Because the Jokka have always roamed." So Darisil said.

Into the sepia shadows went Kediil, to sit by Sedikit's bedside and touch him without any visible fear. She peeled back his lips to examine his gums, stared into his eyes, brushed his forehead, his nose, his sides. "How long has he been sick? Has he eaten? Has he passed waste? Has he vomited? How is his speech when he speaks?" And on and on the questions went. I answered as well as I could. When she'd learned all she deemed necessary, she stood and stretched.

"He may yet live. Bring me a mortar and pestle."

I did so. Throughout the rest of the afternoon and well into the evening, I aided her in the mixture of her medicinals, studying her actions without understanding them. What Kediil knew far surpassed anything I'd ever seen Ikeser do.

"A knife," she said.

I paused.

She bared her teeth at me. "A knife," she repeated.

She slathered the knife I brought her in one of the many pastes she'd made, then turned to Sedikit and poised it over the side of his neck.

When her muscles tensed, I snatched her wrist before she could plunge, almost knocking over the stool to reach her. "What are you doing!"

"His sickness has overwhelmed his body. We must release some of it so he has a chance to finish the fight," she said. Her pupils were vast in the shadows. "Let me do what I must!"

Sedikit's breath hissed below us. His pulse fluttered against his neck too quickly. I released her hand, but I feared anyway.

"Be ready with the bandage," she said, and sliced.

The ordure of decay and infection surged from the wound, following the pus. No blood, save for that which dripped from his skin... I wondered at her skill, to avoid the great vessels in the neck. When she asked, I gave her the bandage and she painted it with yet another poultice before closing the wound and opening the other side. She chose a few more locations on the body—behind his knees and beneath his arms—and then set the knife aside. She checked his forehead and nodded.

I set my hand on Sedikit's head and gaped. "He's cooler!"

"The disease had much advanced," she said as she washed her hands. The cool fragrance of one of her herbs rose from the bowl beneath her fingers, and the sound of the water falling sounded sweetly with the eased breathing of the male. "Earlier I could have treated it with draughts and diet, but so far along there was no choice but to open him." She canted her head. "I will give you the recipe for the draughts, in case anyone else falls ill. You must give them the regimen immediately, or it will do as it has done to this emodo, and you will have to ply the knife."

"I don't think I could," I said, still staggered. The glow beneath Sedikit's skin had re-kindled; even his sleep was easier. "Where did you learn that?"

"Accident," Kediil said with a lopsided smile. "An injury on an already sick male. It does not work for all diseases, but if it will you will be able to feel it with your fingers. There will be lumps . . . hardened ones, if you have waited too long."

"I don't know how to thank you," I said. "Your knowledge is without price."

Kediil found a full smile for me then, but did not answer.

"Serel, you've missed supper—"

Kediil and I both looked up when Darisil stepped through the curtain, his body following his words. Despite the warning, I moved in front of Kediil too late.

"The rumor is true!" the male said, eyes widening. His gaze

found the knife and the bowls and he snarled. "Out! Both of you!"

I thought it wise to obey, if only because an altercation would disturb Sedikit's sleep. I flicked my ear toward the door and Kediil left before me, dropping bags of herbs back in the pouches at her thin belt.

Outside, half the family waited to see what Darisil had been shouting about. Our more spectacular fights had always been viewed as good entertainment, though the family never believed we would remain at odds. One day we would surprise them.

I stood in front of Kediil, waiting to see exactly what part of the situation irritated Darisil the most.

"Are you trying to get us killed?"

That was not what I'd expected. He prowled to and fro before us, so angry his claws showed at the tips of his fingers. The starlight picked them out well enough, though the gathering dusk is one of the hardest times for us to see. "The gods are angry enough with us. They gave us the dry season. They killed Marne's baby and are taking Sedikit. Now you bring this abomination into our home? Are you trying to get us cursed?"

I glanced over my shoulder at Kediil, uneasy. "She is no abomination," I said. "Only another Jokkad like us."

"An anadi who looks half-eperu and has no family? Who wanders wild? I had the stories from the children. Are you mad to bring her here, Serel?"

The family looked disturbed and frightened. I hated when Darisil resorted to such tactics . . . though sometimes, I thought he actually believed his own rhetoric. I straightened and lifted my chin. "She healed Sedikit."

"She took a knife to him!"

"To help his body fight its disease. He is better! Look yourself if you doubt me!"

"Serel... hasn't it occurred to you that if the gods are cuffing us for our disobedience, stopping their hand will only make them angrier?"

I stared at him. "You don't truly believe this is the work of the Trinity, do you?"

"Trifold."

"Whatever!" I said, exasperated. "Bad luck! Coincidence! We will weather it as we've weathered everything."

"Will we?" he asked. He glanced from me to Kediil, then said to the watchers, "Come. It is past time to rest." And he led them into the house, leaving me in the deepening dark with my peculiar half-eperu anadi and her magic potions. I turned to her, chagrined, finding her expression resigned and her eyes darker than the starlight would have them.

"An old story," I guessed.

"The oldest," she answered, her voice soft. "That which is different is threatening."

I touched her wrist. "I would have thought to offer you something for your work... truly, I would have liked you to stay, if your wandering feet could have been stilled."

Her brows lifted. "And invite the displeasure of the gods?"

"I have never been much for religion," I said. "And I have always been more interested in the mind beneath a body."

She tilted her head, cupped my shoulders in her hands. "And

that is why you want so much to stay in one place, is it? Because you sorrow to see the breeders lose their minds to exertion, toil and heat. You must know that staying in one place will bring its own hardships?"

"Of course," I said. "But a new danger may be an easier one." I smiled. "We make of life what we can."

Kediil searched my eyes—an unmistakable examination, her own gaze unblinking and bright. Her eyes had a beautiful color, a green-blue that suggested deep water. She withdrew her hands and took a deep breath. The packets she handed to me were fragrant with the scent of life.

"I would like to have stayed and mixed these properly, but they will do some good as long as they're ground. They should help."

She turned then and walked away. I fingered the packets, breathing their clean, sharp fragrance, then called, "You could visit. I could meet you in the hills, tell you how our grand experiment goes . . . this settled life."

Kediil grinned. "Perhaps in a year your children will see my fire in these parts again."

"I look forward to it," I said, and she left.

For a long time I stood there with the herbs in my hand. Thinking of how old the stars were that gave light to my eyes, how many Jokka had stood beneath the purple sky with the heat of the summer on their skins and the weight of tradition on their shoulders.

I thought how nice it was to be one of those who did not feel the burden.

With the packets in my hand, I went to tend to Sedikit.

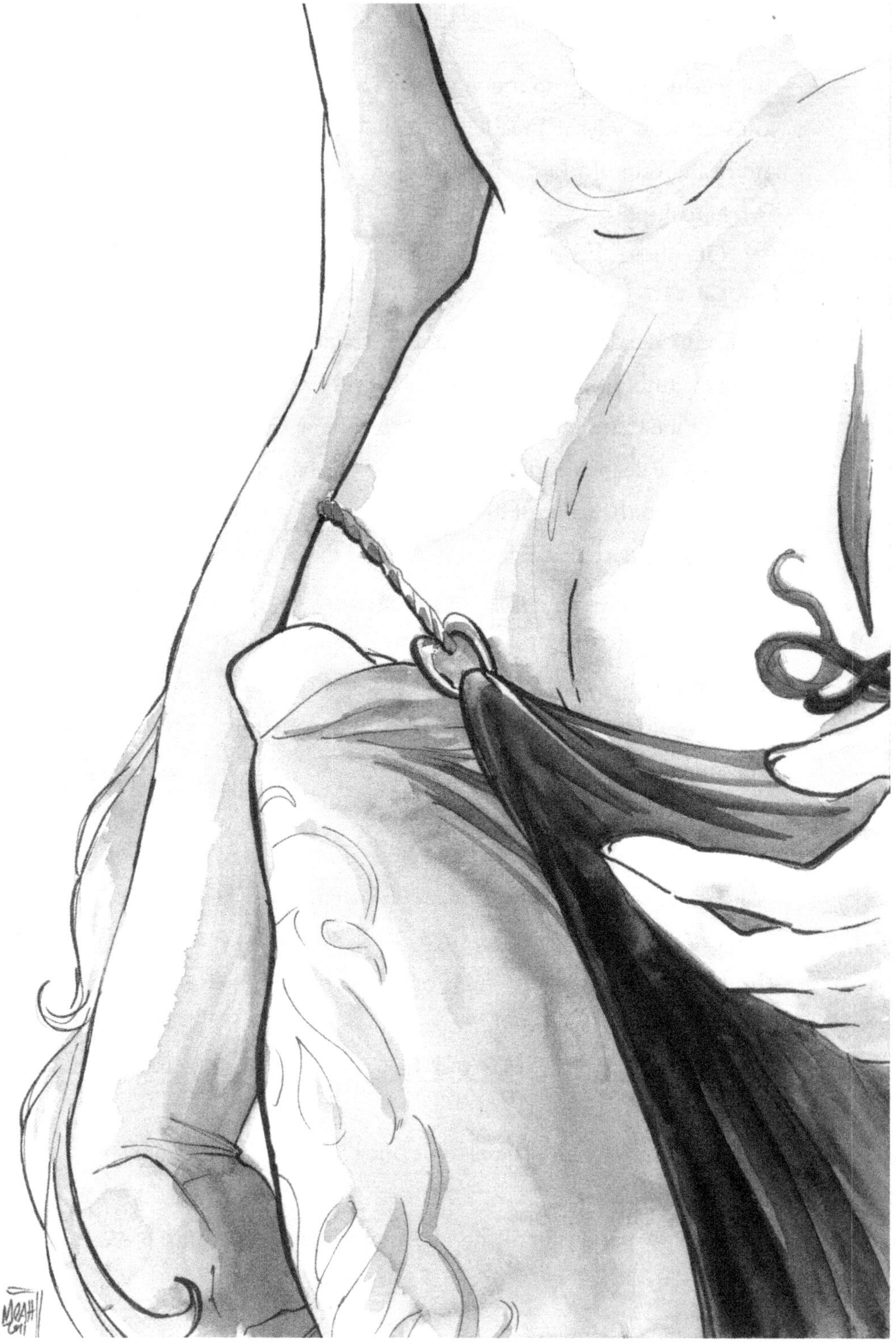

A Trifold Spiral Knot

Void: Erdiil

When the sun has not yet woken but the night is threatened in the east, the sky is a sublime and fragile purple, heavy with age and darkness. It carries with it the multi-hued gleam of fading stars. It is tired by defeat. It is fleeing the spectacle of dawn.

That color is the color of my eyes.

The color currently shading my ribs is a different kind of fragile purple, a thin translucent one shivering with hot sunlight. It is thrown by a prayer fan held upright by sand-weakened soil. Stripes of red and tree-blood yellow border the translucent purple panes. The fan's handle casts a violet shadow, nearing black. By midday, the shadow will have compacted into a black so dense it seems to deny the sunlight.

This is the color of my skin, the pooled and active blackness of truedark, of lack of sight. The sun puzzles at my edges. It seeks to illumine the spirals that decorate other Jokka and does not find them, for I am unmarked. It is the reason my clan sent me away to serve the gods. Since I was old enough to hear and understand, I have known it: I am the Void's. Snuffer of stars, bringer of silence, the calm of nothingness. The Void is male, but no one ever speaks of His children.

The sand beneath my shoulders and hips is still cool. By midday, it will burn.

WORLD: Mayiin

My toe pads didn't touch dust in Dardenil until late morning; I'd hitched a ride with a clan heading north until they'd reached the forest stand, and then we'd parted company. Since then it had been me, my aching feet, my determination... and now, my destination.

My sojourns in the south had taught me what to expect of the town: a handful of rough buildings made of mud brick and thatched with sun-burnt grass, a well, and communal beast-keep. The number of buildings varied as you travelled, but for the most part decreased as you headed north: most of the larger permanent towns were still near Sarel's, who had started this crazy-wondrous thing. Permanent living places! Surely Sarel had gorged on too many truedark tales.

I wished I could have met it.

Still, I had a mission of my own, and I'd spent most of two years pursuing it. At long last, Dardenil stretched in front of my aching toes: Dardenil, the only town that had built a temple to honor the gods. Dardenil, with its secret treasure, the one I'd needed most of a year just to name.

The Jokka sitting in the shade of the houses looked

prosperous. I saw no anadi, no doubt all hidden in their special rooms beneath the ground, but emodo and eperu I saw in plenty. Both males and neuters wore precious gems and shaped and painted clay medallions in their manes, and the neuters wore clothing painted with colorful swirls.

I stopped the nearest one, a wiry eperu with delicate features and skin the shimmering gold of sand beneath an early afternoon sun. "Pardon, ke eperu, but do you have a moment for a footsore traveller?"

"Of course," it said, brown brows lifting.

"The temple," I said. "I've walked far to see it."

It smiled then, and pointed between the houses. "Keep going," it said. "It's by the pond."

I thanked it and followed the route. A frisson of pleasure and dread ran through my body. So close at last to my goal. What would it be like, to finally reach it?

Around the corner from the last building in Dardenil I found myself enfolded in beauty: a low building of rich tawny brick on the bank of a pond that blazed the blue of the summer sky. Trees and brush lined the edge of the pond and shrouded the building in fronds of water-rich green, and where the foliage leaned too far over the water it reflected its verdant boughs. Truly the gods could be worshipped here.

And yet as I approached, I saw that the pond and its greenery were isolated. No streams ran from this peaceful place. The plains encroached on its borders, caging it in waving yellow grasses.

I shivered for an entirely different reason and entered the building.

❧ ☙

Void: Erdiil

The sky is an interesting case. Some Jokka say our first color terms evolved to describe the sky. It's true that we have beautiful words for all the many moods of the firmament. The rarest of these words evoke the sky in its vast emptiness, untouched by the graduations of light shed by the rising and falling heavenly bodies, by the refraction and dilution of clouds. Such words whisper to the spirit of stagnation, of moments trapped outside of time, of context.

No color is without change, except the color of the cloudless sky at midday, and the sky at truedark's hour. Today, as I lie beneath it, the sky is *neide*, a word ancient in its cadence. A *neide* sky is empty, like me. It is stagnant, like me.

I was born emodo—male—which is one of the reasons I was chosen to serve the Void: I was not just unmarked but also the right sex. But at my first puberty, I Turned anadi, and there were many hushed conferences about what that meant, that the Void would Turn his chosen vessel female. The others discussed it at length, and decided in the end that it was meant as confirmation of their plan.

The individuals who serve the gods exist thus far on the sufferance of the community. The other Jokka feed and clothe us, helped us build our temple. We are in a time of plenty, and they are happy to please the gods by aiding us. But plentiful times never last. Planning for the harder years, the gods' servants had thought of breeding and offering their children in return for the support of the townspeople. My Turning female was the sign they'd sought. I was to be the first.

It is never assured that you will Turn at either puberty, but if you do, it's more likely at your first. No one told me it would hurt. Do not imagine a ripping pain. It is an ache that throbs through your hips as your bones widen. Your belly rounds. Your back strains as your spine settles into a deeper curve. Developing breasts is almost an afterthought: you hunger for certain foods, and the more you eat the more your breasts swell. But it's nothing to the reshaping of bone in your hips, and that ache doesn't begin to address the mental distress of watching your genital pouch shrink back into your skin.

Months pass, and finally one day you rest your hand on your belly and feel a quivering inside yourself. It is stillness and emptiness, but the kind that is awaiting motion. Not at all like the sky at midday.

Not at all like my belly now.

WORLD: Mayiin

"Welcome, ke eperu," an anadi said as I entered. I glanced at her, startled at the sweetness of her voice and the precision of her enunciation. I had lost the habit of expecting anadi to speak clearly: I'd seen too many in my travels who'd lost their minds to the exertion on the trail, to heat, to pregnancy . . . all the things that afflict the breeders anyway, and anadi in particular. Perhaps there was hope for what I sought, then.

"Thank you," I said, then took a deep breath. Suddenly words were hard. Hope was hard. "Is . . . I'm looking for Erdiil. Is she here?"

"'She'?" the anadi repeated, then laughed sadly. Her eyes were the color of sun-browned leaves, rich but hot. "You have not spoken with Erdiil in some time, I see." She touched her throat, ears drooping.

"What is it?" I asked, throttling a sense of desperation. "Is she hurt?"

"It has gone into the plains to pray," the anadi said.

"Is that... she's neuter, now? What does that mean, going to the plains to pray? Will it be back soon?"

"We don't know," the anadi said. She had lost her gaiety altogether, and I sensed sorrow in her scent and the droop of her head, just ever-so-slightly forward. "The Void has rejected Erdiil, after we thought we understood why it Turned female at first puberty."

I looked around. There was no place to sit: no furniture in fact in this antechamber save the narrow brick table that separated us. I rested my hands on it. "I don't understand. He Turned female, which is a frightening fate, and then at second puberty, she Turned neuter, and now... now everyone is upset? Eperu is better!"

The anadi stared at me calmly until I dropped my head and blushed white. "I'm sorry," I said. "I didn't mean to insult."

"The gods love us in all our shapes," the anadi said, then went on, "Erdiil Turned in order to fulfill our need to give the community a child in return for supplies and food. When she Turned neuter, we lost the certainty of the god's approval. Erdiil is seeking meaning in the sun. It will return when it has been absolved."

Which to my ears sounded like a fine way to commit suicide; we neuters may be the sturdiest of the sexes, but that doesn't mean we should go throw ourselves on the sand and let the sun bake our brains out. And absolution for what? "Which way did it go?" I asked.

The anadi frowned. "Pardon?"

"Which way did it go?" I repeated, more slowly. "I came a long way to talk to Erdiil and I'm not going away until I do."

Perplexed, the anadi pointed westerly.

"Thank you," I said and turned to go. On a whim, I stopped and withdrew a few strips of jerky. I set them on the brick table. "For the Jokka who serve the gods."

"Thank you," she said, still apparently uncertain of me.

I stepped out of the temple, and then forged my way out of the oasis of green and blue. The transition from water-fed foliage to sun-crisped grass was abrupt, and I spread my paws until I felt the hot ground between each toe. To my travel-trained eyes, Erdiil's track through the fields stood apart from the surroundings, a brighter trail of broken grass reflecting the sun, white on gold. I set off in pursuit.

Void: Erdiil

Light itself has colors . . . which is how we tell time. The hours are named for the changing light of the sun as it travels, and how it interacts with the light of the moon if it's risen. It is now the hour between white and copper, when the light is most white while still holding elements of the descending sun. This is a single word: *akiiñel*.

There is also a single word for the two hours before midday, the midday hour, and the two hours after, the most dangerous parts of the day: *kushuleñe*. The hours with fangs. Madness stalks all Jokka: the anadi are the easiest prey, with the emodo following and eperu the hardest of all. And madness has many claws: exertion, pregnancy, over-excitement, age . . . extremes of temperature. If Madness has a foot like a Jokkad, then temperature is its smallest toe claw, and pregnancy, the ultimate of life's expected exertions, is the killing thumb claw. But in summer, exposed, during the *kushuleñe*, even an eperu might fall beneath the littlest claw.

I courted insanity.

I did it purposefully. I hadn't expected to change at second puberty. I had been prepared to offer a child to serve the Void. The spark inside me had quivered, waiting only for the seed to take root. I had loved being emodo, but once I'd Turned I welcomed the fecundity of my body.

Turning neuter from female is painless and almost unnoticeable. Your breasts melt away. Your hips remain the same size. And then one day you bleed for a few days, and when it's done your body has sealed the last ingress into your womb, and your breath comes easier, and your body begins to build muscle, and walking is a pleasure.

The spark in your womb dies, leaving the emptiness of the midday sky. No life will come of me.

So I waited for the fang and claw of the hours of death. Waited with outstretched arms, on my back with my belly exposed to the sky's cruelty. The heat had long since sunk deep into my flesh.

Surely it wouldn't be long now.

It was the hour *akiiñel*, so I didn't understand the blue shadow that fell over me like a wet cloth. I looked up and squinted, and saw a Jokkad standing at my feet, staring into my eyes. It took several moments for my eyes to cease their watering, and then I saw this person clearly: an eperu, pale as living blood, shimmering, unmarked. It had a white mane and tail longer than any I'd ever seen. Dust and grass had stained its legs and chest, and burrs were tangled in its tail.

Its eyes were the color of the first hour of dusk, that wavering lilac that we adore, for it presages the hours of safety, of cool.

"Who are you?" I asked. "And why have you interrupted my prayer?"

"I am Mayiin," the other said, in a voice that sounded familiar. "I was sired by your father, and our mother carried us both in the womb at the same time."

At last, the hours in the sun touched my mind, dizzied me. "Why does that matter?"

It dropped to its knees beside me and grabbed a water bag. One hand slid behind my head and held it up, and it poured the fluid past my parched lips. "It just does. Drink."

World: Mayiin

Had I come so far only to lose it? When I'd discovered halfway through my journey that Erdiil had Turned female I'd resigned myself to finding her dull in spirit, a resignation that had fled when the anadi had told me the news in the temple. I fought my fear as I moved Erdiil's too hot head onto my lap. Cradling it in one arm, I reached over and jerked the prayer fan out of the sand, retrenching it closer and twisting it so that it gave us some paltry shade.

I returned my attention to the face of this creature, this treasure I'd spent so many years seeking. We Jokka gave little thought to the anadi who bore us, for it was the eperu of our clans who raised us. Nor did we have any special claim on our sires, for the patriarch of the clan was our disciplinarian, and made all the decisions for its members. The clans traded Jokka of similar age whenever they met another group with like individuals, for only thus could we bring new blood to the clan.

We never knew what happened to the Jokka we grew up with, for inevitably we parted ways. The anadi who bore us were nameless. The clan was everything.

But I ... oh, I remembered Erdiil. I remembered how strange we were, the pair of us: Erdiil the darkness of the Void, and me the vivid brilliance of blood. Erdiil had been born male, and I female: the right colors for the right sexes to serve the gods. But unlike Erdiil, I had a single mark, a tied spiral knot just beneath the slit of my navel. My imperfection had separated us.

For many years I walked, surrounded by others but alone, traded here and there until I Turned emodo, and then unexpectedly eperu at the last. The more I wandered, leading a rikka with my tent and all my worldly possessions, the more incomplete I felt. When I curled up on my rugs to sleep, I realized I was waiting for someone else to mirror me, his head to my knees, his knees to my forehead, a spiral curl of blood and darkness. Slowly, I reassembled my memory of Erdiil, and knew

I had to find him.

Which is how I discovered that Jokka are easily lost, switching members among clans as we do so frequently. For two years I traveled, asking after a Jokkad colored like Erdiil. For two years I searched in vain, because before Sarel had thought up the idea of settling in permanent towns, serving the gods had meant being sent to one of many traveling clans composed of mostly those dedicated to the service of the gods. Two years of my life, and my goal was shivering in my lap with heat fever.

"I will not let you die," I hissed as I wet a cloth and pressed it to Erdiil's forehead. "I will not!"

Void: Erdiil

I didn't recognize the strange eperu until it set my head in its lap. Some memory stirred, in the dark places too deep for words to find. I remembered the feel of those thighs. No, the smell of them, beneath the grass and sweat. Was I too young to have Turned again? Or was I dying in the grasses behind a temple?

"You're dying in the grasses behind a temple." Words superimposed on distant thunder. I struggled to open my eyes and my entire body thrashed in a horror so deep only my body could answer it.

The Snuffer of Stars stood before me. All His servants had lied. He was not a Jokkad the black of truedark. He was an abyssal emptiness only faintly shaped like a person, with empty eye sockets and nostrils that gaped as if ripped open. His mane and tail, and the hair at the fringes of His wrists and ankles, quested blindly at the air and ground near His body, consuming whatever it touched.

I tried to scramble away from Him, but my body remained too weak, cradled in the arms of a figure now bleached and surreal. I turned my face, but I could still see Him, even with my eyes closed.

"I'm supposed to only go mad," I said. "It wasn't in my plan to die completely. If I live, someone can use my body for labor."

"Just as your body was supposed to be used in my service."

I shivered. "It was not me who Turned from you!"

"Your death will serve me better than your living." He stepped forward. His feet were as articulated as hands, and from each toe a wicked claw protruded, digging furrows into the soil. I moaned and twisted, trying to flee.

WORLD: Mayiin

Erdiil writhed against me, burning flesh pressed against my legs, and then jerked away. My only consolation was that it clung to me in its fever. I kept dampening its face and throat and chest, when it was still enough.

"You aren't supposed to die," I told Erdiil when it stiffened and stared at the sky. I swallowed, trying to wet my tongue and fangs. "Do you hear me? Not until I have a name for what you are to me, and even not even then."

"Belong to the Void," Erdiil whispered.

"No," I said, folding over to hold it between my chest and lap. "You've been emodo, anadi and eperu, all three. You don't belong to the Void. You belong to me!"

Void: Erdiil

A white foot stepped between me and the Void's black foot. I froze and stared up at this newcomer, thrown into such sharp relief against the darkness of the god.

"The eperu is mine." A voice like the wind through a field of grasses, that broad, that soft, that many multitudes.

At first I thought my savior was the Brightness, the anadi goddess of the sun. But when I focused on the new shape, I could find no breasts. No, there were breasts, and then there were none. And sometimes the newcomer was male. It—he—she? Flickered between all the sexes with every rise and fall of its chest. Not the Brightness then, nor the World for all its windsong voice: the World was only neuter. Who was this creature, then, with its body pale as blood and its hair as bright as dawn? Whoever it was, the Void did not like it.

"This eperu is mine," the Void said. "It is of more use in death than in life."

"Not so," the stranger said, and beneath the windsong I heard a familiar voice, echoing the words.

"Then madness, so it can be used for labor."

"No," the newcomer said again. "This eperu is mine."

"I will not suffer this creature to live in freedom. I stole its marks before birth. It belongs to me."

"This creature belongs to life," the stranger said, ears folding all the way down. "To light, to laughter and language, to understanding, to exploration, to the illumination of every Jokku soul."

Such an amazing charter. In wonder, I whispered, "Who are you?"

The stranger turned to me, then crouched, one hand steadying it against the ground. It had eyes the pale blue of milk. "I am the first Jokkad who was *elithik*, who was all three sexes. I am the last. I am all the Jokka in between."

"Like me," I whispered.

"Like you," it said, except now it was male. "Because there is virtue in every sex, but only those who have experienced them all can convince the rest."

"This Jokkad belongs to me," said the thunder, but it was receding, like a storm that was rolling back from the sky.

"This Jokkad belongs to itself," said the stranger. "And, if it will, to me. Do you, Erdiil? Do you will it?"

How I'd longed to bear a child. How I'd sorrowed to lose my manhood. How I yearned to bear some burden now that my shoulders had the strength for it.

How strange those thoughts had been, so strange I'd dared not voice them.

"Yes," I whispered. "Oh yes. I'm yours."

It took my hands and licked them with a cool tongue. Then it did the same to my face, my cheeks. Every lap banished the fear, the heat, a tendril of the Void.

"Mine own," said the stranger. "Lover of the trifold virtues."

WORLD: Mayiin

The fang-sharp ache of tormented muscle woke me from the sleep I hadn't remembered entering. I'd twisted to one side to keep from suffocating Erdiil, and there I'd failed in my vigil. It was well after dusk. I despaired. I'd argued with the eperu's fevered whispers for as long as I'd had strength, but in the end its madness had outlasted me.

And yet, the head in my lap was warm, not hot. When I found the courage to peek, it was gazing up at me.

"You look like someone I know," Erdiil said.

I started laughing. "Well I should! We shared a womb!"

"Does that matter?" it asked, but it was smiling in . . . wonder? Tenderness?

"Yes," I said. "It does. It makes us . . . something to one another. Something I have no word for."

"Womb-doubles?" Erdiil said with a breathy laugh. "Grain seeds from the same pod? Jokka like the stars that circle one another in the sky? There are thousands and thousands of words, but there isn't any word for that."

"We'll have to make one up," I said.

"I guess you're meant to stay with me," Erdiil said.

"Yes," I answered, despite finding its statement strangely phrased. "I need someone to finish my circle when I sleep. I can find some place to work in Dardenil while you live in the temple—"

"I'm not going back to the temple," Erdiil said. It struggled to lift itself from the ground and I helped it, worried. Before it could say anything else, I handed it the water bag. Clear beads of liquid dripped from its chin as it drank, and then it looked down and its ears flipped down.

I followed its gaze to the knot of gray on its belly. "You're marked!"

"You have a mark like this," Erdiil whispered.

I pulled the waist of my pants down so it could see—no, not just see. So it could confirm the memory.

"I don't belong to the Void," my double whispered.

"No," I said. "You belong to us."

It glanced at me sharply. "We have work to do . . . Mayiin."

"Work we can do together?" I asked cheerfully.

Erdiil laughed and said. "Yes."

"Good enough," I said. I studied its eyes with care. "You're certain you're well?"

It met my gaze, ears splayed. "Well enough. And you? You're certain you want anything to do with me? You don't know me very well."

"I know you in my blood, and you know me in yours," I said with satisfaction. "We'll do your work, and we'll make up the word for sharing the same blood and the same womb, and having been born of the same seed."

"And decide why that matters," Erdiil said.

I wrapped my hand around its arm—gently, since it had been so lately fevered—and said in a low voice, "It matters because I missed you like another part of my heart. Because my soul never forgot you. And now it will matter because we will be clan to one another."

"A strange clan, of people who are of the same blood!"

I nodded. "Very strange. So now I'll ask: will you want anything to do with me?"

Erdiil canted its head, touched a finger to my nose. "There must be something to your strange idea," it said with a soft laugh, "because I trust you as if I've always known you. So yes. Let's go do the work."

I grinned and bounced to my feet, helping it up. "So what is this work, anyway?"

Erdiil's eyes had a secret sparkle. "We're going to teach the Jokka the virtues of every sex. That there's as much honor and beauty in being anadi as there is in being eperu or emodo. That all of them should be equal in the eyes of a Jokkad."

I stepped back, ears flattening in alarm. "Surely you don't mean that. Of course, we need the anadi and the emodo and their roles are sacred, but . . . who wouldn't want to be eperu?"

"There is beauty in being emodo," Erdiil began.

"I can see that," I interrupted. "At least you get to keep your mind longer."

Erdiil reached for my hands and took them, turning them in its. My fingers remained as short as they had been at birth, though work had given them more strength. Erdiil's were long and delicate and powerful, still the hands of an emodo. "Have you considered that there's more to life than being smart?"

I stared at it. Perhaps the sun had baked Erdiil's brain after all. "What more could there be? How can you enjoy anything without understanding it? Without . . . without a way for others to explain it to you? Without . . ."

". . . without a name?" Erdiil asked, dawn-purple eyes sparkling.

Exasperated, I said, "That's different."

"Is it?" The eperu touched my chin. "You sought me on the strength of something no Jokkad can name. I, too, have something in me that has no name, and it is the joy at the thought of bearing children, the pleasure of an open womb, the ability to spark life in others."

"But you don't . . ." I stopped abruptly. If Erdiil missed those things, reminding it that it could no longer have them was cruel, wasn't it? The thought boggled.

"Can you see the edges of it?" Erdiil asked.

I tried. I had been anadi once, but I'd been too young for thoughts of childbirth. Still, if I forced myself, I could remember something . . . a sense that I could receive the world and hold it in me longer. Perhaps that's why anadi fell so easily to the perils of the world: they were built to welcome it. And to be emodo . . . well, what would it be like to sire children?

What had it been like to be our sire? To lose your children?

I let my head dip forward until my cheek rested against Erdiil's shoulder.

"You do see!" Erdiil whispered.

I did. I licked my lips and said, hushed, "Teaching Jokka to value those things . . . such a work will take a while."

My double, my womb-mate, my other-self born to me like the stars that circle one another in the sky, said, "It will never be done. That's the best kind of work."

TRIFOLD: Erdiil

Shadows cast by cool stones in moonlight are a favorable gray. Shadow colors of all kind are favorites among us, for light and heat are infrequently kind, but the night shadows are best-loved of all, and the words we use for the subtle colored ones are often used in poetry when we speak of ease, of relief, of refuge.

That color is the color of the knot on my belly, placed there a strange god who looks a great deal like my new companion.

I look up at the sky and I laugh, and then I pick my way after Mayiin, to begin what will never be finished.

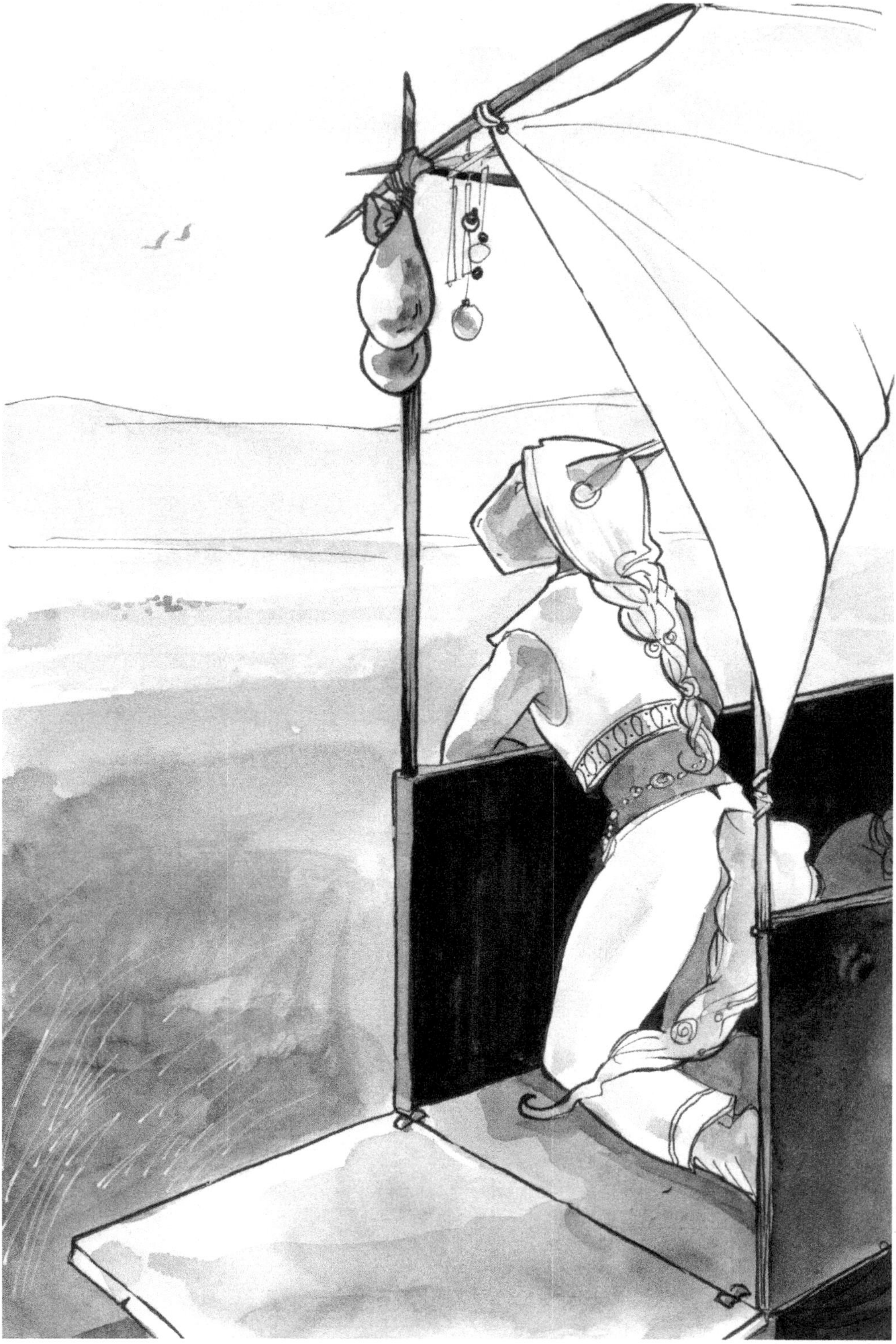

Money for Sorrow, Made Joy

The houses of Het Ikoped were only a few days distant when Ledin, the caravan master, called us to the fire pit before supper. I arrived before the others and helped Ledin set up the stakes for the lanterns. Purple shadows stretched from our feet, for the twilight in summer came reluctantly and full of color. I liked the palette: orange sky, violet shadows, black hills in silhouette at the horizon's edge. Here in the north, colors are cleaner, steadier.

With the lanterns casting yellowed light and the fire, new-built, casting orange, the two of us sat to await the others. I glanced at Ledin; its composure crafted a mask of its face, but its dark green eyes glittered. I knew then that this would be the night, and I grinned.

One by one the rest of the caravan joined us: sturdy eperu, neuters, the only sex of the Jokka that could withstand the grueling travel of a trade caravan. Last of all came little Thodi, our orphan found two circuits back.

Thodi wiggled around to sit by me, resting its slim head on my shoulder. I realized, bemused, that it had grown.

"Friends," Ledin said, tufted ears canted forward, "you've known for a while that I had more planned for our venture than simple trade. Tonight, at last, I think we are ready for the plan." It withdrew from its pouch a folded square of cloth; with great drama, Ledin opened it and displayed it for view—a map of the known continent, which when seen thus demonstrated just how little we Jokka knew of our land. "I want to explore the northwestern region."

The others leaned forward, and the fire jumped to their eyes. I knew mine held a similar flame. Exploration? To see places not seen before? Feel perhaps a cooler breeze than the ones on the sandy soil beneath us now? To touch foot to places no Jokkad had ever walked? I had never heard of anyone taking up such a charter. Jokka did not travel.

"We are approaching Het Ikoped," Ledin continued, placing the map on the ground and anchoring it with a few stones. "I propose this het be our base. We will buy supplies there for a year's travel and go where we can before we have to turn back."

"Why only a year?" someone asked.

My ears tilted backward. "Because we have only enough shell for a year's supplies," I offered. I saw Ledin nod. I was the only eperu in the caravan besides Ledin itself who had an interest in money, and so I helped with our finances. We were not a rich caravan, and supplies for a year, unless carefully chosen, would bankrupt us.

"Anyway, we will return in a year, take on cargo, and run the trade route for more shell before returning to resume exploring. I am hoping we will discover resources on the journey that will enable us to take fewer supplies on the next run, but we cannot make assumptions. We will be the first." Ledin sat back, resting its slender hands on its knees. "What say you all?"

They hardly needed to answer: the hunger in their faces and the way they leaned almost into the fire said enough.

Ledin laughed. "Very well, then. Let's make food and get back on the road!"

The eperu scattered, chattering amongst themselves . . . leaving me there with Ledin and Thodi.

"You well, little one?" I asked it, ears tilting toward it.

Thodi wrapped its arms around my waist, rubbed its chin on my shoulder. "I can hardly believe it, Ekanoi! Since I've been with the caravan, you've been taking me places I've never seen. But now to be taken places that *no one* has seen?" It shivered. "This is happiness!"

Ledin heard and chuckled. "It may be that Jokka have passed that way before, Thodi. Indeed, it may be that Jokka have touched foot and hand to every span of this continent. But if so, we haven't heard of it. And everyone knows that Jokka do not—"

"—travel," Thodi finished, and grinned. Its face had a fineness of feature reminiscent of a male, one which had prompted not a little conjecture among the others over what sex Thodi had originally been . . . and what sex Thodi would become. Its first puberty was probably several years past already. "But look at us! *We* travel!"

"Caravans trade," I corrected. "Travel implies no reason for the journey. There are no idle journeys. Only caravans and trade."

"So we trade. Still we move places." Thodi played with the chain of striped brown pebbles and tarnished silver at my waist. "What will we bring back, ke Ledin? Will we make maps?"

"That we will," Ledin said. "And we will bring back whatever is beautiful and useful." It stood, brushed off its thighs, then bent down and touched the child's sloped nose. "Maybe we will find something of such great value we will be able to return to the towns and put down a stone to found our own House . . . a House of such riches we will doze-dream on piles of shell."

Thodi giggled. "But why would we want to stay in one place?"

"That's a good question," Ledin said.

"Some of us could stay at the House and doze in the piles of shell," I said. "The rest of us would run the caravan. Then, when the caravan comes back, we'd switch. . . ."

Thodi pressed its hand to its mouth. "That's silly."

"Yes," I said.

And, "Who can know the future?" from Ledin, who ran a hand through my mane before saying, "Enjoy the evening."

The two of us remained before the fire. I idly stroked Thodi's soft, dark curls; it continued playing with my waist-chain. "Do you think I can do something brave and useful on the journey?" it asked me.

"Like what?" I asked.

"I don't know. I could catch so much food for us off the trail that we don't need to touch our stores at all? Or maybe help defend the wagons from marauding beasts!"

"Marauding beasts, is it?" I said, laughing. I ran my finger down its nose. "Why would you want to get in the way of such things? I bet they're large and hairy and mean."

"Like the anadi!" Thodi crowed.

"And how do you know what the females are like?" I asked, amused. "You've probably never seen one."

"I would if you let me go with you and Ledin into town," the child said, frowning.

"Probably not," I said. "We usually talk to the males. They run the Houses. Besides, how else could we protect you from the anadi's dripping fangs?" I feigned a pounce, baring my own fangs.

Thodi snorted. "Anadi poison is a truedark tale!"

"Are you sure?" I asked, all innocence.

It frowned at me. "Aren't you?"

I grinned. "I don't know. I'm not anadi."

Thodi shivered. "Me neither! Thank the World. Females don't have any fun!"

Ah, bald truth. "So why do you want to wound yourself in the brave defense of the caravan, little one?"

"I was hoping to earn my ring soon," it said, looking up at the silvery hoop hanging from my left ear.

I chuckled. "You know we can't give you a ring until after your second puberty, or you'd have one already."

"But I could have already gone through my second puberty, and not known it!"

I hugged it and sighed. "You must be patient, ba Thodi. You will know when you're not a child any longer."

It wiggled in my arms, then deflated, resting its cheek against my flat chest. "I guess so."

"You should go help Mekena with supper, ah? It's your turn tonight."

Thodi nodded and drew itself to its feet. It had an almost anadi-like obedience . . . something for which I was thankful, if also somewhat concerned. Shaking my head, I rose and ambled back to my wagon. We'd be rolling in an hour or so, and the creak in the right wheel would soon drive me sun-crazy if I didn't fix it now.

I stopped inside the store to savor the flat floors for a few minutes. At no point on its year-long circuit did the caravan traverse anything but broken road and uneven ground. The general store in Het Ikoped had stone tile floors, cool and smooth against my callused toes.

Perhaps youth was blind to such subtle pleasures, for Thodi trotted past me and began poking into barrels and glancing into bins.

"Ba Thodi, be careful, ah?" I said, proceeding to the back counter. The emodo there wore his tan mane in a handsome braid, and his clear purple eyes rested on me with polite interest. His light tunic covered most of his skin, but what I could see of it was a supple dark brown with lighter spirals. "Good afternoon, ke emodo."

"And to you, ke eperu," he said. "May I help you?"

"Ke Ledin's caravan just came into town," I said. "We were wondering if you were interested in barter?"

"I might be," he said. "Your caravan is outside?"

"Indeed."

He nodded. "I will talk with your caravan master, then. What were you hoping to trade for?"

"I'm not sure yet," I said, glancing around the store. "I would appreciate some time to make a list."

The male smiled. "Please, take as much time as you need. I will be outside."

I nodded, watched him walk out, then pulled out one of the three slates the caravan owned. The piece of stone in my hand had cost half a trunk of furs—somewhat expensive, but far less than one of the specially treated slabs of wood would have been. With a thin sliver of chalk in my hand, I drifted through the store, noting what would be useful for the journey. Grain and dried fruit. Dried meat. Fire-coals and tinder, soap, fat for cooking, fodder for the animals. . . . The tally grew.

I sat on a trunk with the slate and rubbed my head.

"Bad, Ekanoi?" Thodi said, thumping onto the trunk beside me.

"Difficult," I said. "We will have to unload everything we brought at an excellent price to afford all that we'd need for a year's journey. The grain is more expensive than it should be."

"Is he cheating us?" Thodi asked, eyes wide.

"No. . . . Probably something happened this year. Bad harvest, or a caravan missed this het." I shook my head. "Come on. Let's go talk to Ledin."

Thodi followed me out to the caravans. We passed the emodo on the way, and I did not like his obvious cheer. I reached Ledin's wagon and glanced inside. "Ledin?"

"In here, Ekanoi."

I climbed onto the platform, helping Thodi up after me. Ledin was seated on one of the trunks, a slate resting on its lap and one hand tangled in its mane.

"We will not have enough, will we," I said.

Ledin shook its head.

I took the slate and glanced at the numbers. My tail twitched. "Is that all? This is barely more than we paid for it."

"I had to sell, quickly," Ledin said with a sigh. "I heard at the wayfarer's house that Batasil's caravan is only a day away."

I grimaced. Batasil could have dozed atop a pile of shell had it chosen to; it preferred instead to trade, and had twice the number of wagons we had, full of luxury goods that commanded such exorbitant prices it could afford to sell its basic goods at cost. Ledin was right: we could not compete with Batasil.

Yet the prices on the two slates missed one another by two wagons' worth of goods.

Thodi looked from Ledin's face to mine. "Does this mean we're not going?"

"No . . . ," Ledin said. "Just that we will come back in half a year instead of a year." It smiled and cuffed Thodi lightly on the shoulder. "Sa, what's with that face? At least we'll have a party tomorrow night. Batasil throws wondrous parties."

That was the final injustice: that hating Batasil was impossible. Its affable nature and easy generosity with what it considered its fraternity of neuter traders precluded hatred. I finally found a wry chuckle. "That it does. Shall I go buy half a year's supplies, then?"

Ledin nodded.

Thodi followed me off the wagon. "Ekanoi! Half a year? That's nothing! We'll barely get into the wilderness!"

I waited for it to catch up to me, then rested my arm over its shoulders. "We have no choice, little one. We can only stretch our shell so far."

"But can't we borrow some? Maybe from Batasil?"

"Ke Batasil to you, little one. Be polite. And no, we can't borrow money from Batasil. We would spend too long paying it when we got back."

"Why?"

I rubbed my forehead, wondering just how much to explain about the worth of shell over time. "Because we would have to pay it more than we borrowed, because that would be shell Batasil wouldn't have while we had it."

"Ke Batasil has other money though, so what does it matter?"

I laughed. "Just trust me, ba Thodi. Borrowing money will only make us poorer."

Thodi sighed and leaned against me. "I was so excited."

"Ba eperu, listen to me," I said. I stopped, faced it and rested my hands on its shoulders. "We're still going. We're just coming back a little sooner than expected, that's all. Understand?"

Thodi rolled a lip between its teeth, then nodded, ears splaying.

"Good. Now you start looking forward to that party, ah? Batasil is going to have things to eat and drink so exotic you won't remember their names in the morning. A real adult's party."

One tufted ear pricked up. "Really? An adult's party?"

"I promise."

Thodi hugged me tightly. I rested my chin on its head, chuckling softly. "Come on. Those supplies want purchase."

"Okay!"

The other eperu helped me roll the barrels from the general store to our caravans while the emodo supervised the transfer of goods. By late evening he stood with me and I counted into his hand the balance of our payment while Ledin watched. We marked our tokens and exchanged them, marked them again to record the transaction . . . and then Ledin and I turned to our wagons, half of them empty and the other half carrying our supplies.

"And that," Ledin said, "is the beginning of our venture."

I handed it the transaction token and chuckled. "May the Brightness, Void, and World bless us all."

"But mostly the World," Ledin said, grinning. It squeezed my shoulder, then padded into the purple dark.

Batasil's caravan rolled into town the following day, bringing with it clouds of amber dust. I watched with Thodi from the vantage of Feda's wagon, the one with the perch built above the frame. Feda had sacrificed the mobility of the sails built onto every wagon frame to have that perch, but it commanded a spectacular view. Thodi and I arranged the remaining sails to give us as much shade as possible, and sat there well over an hour while Batasil's wagons crawled into town.

"They're big," Thodi muttered.

I nodded. Our wagons had been built to the standard trade size; only a few businesses made them. Batasil made its own rules, though. "Big and full of strange things. Maybe we can get it to show you some of its rarer goods."

Both of Thodi's ears perked. "That would be fun."

I grinned and tickled its side. "After the party, though. We'll leave tomorrow night, so maybe tomorrow in the afternoon."

"Then I guess I'll take a nap now," Thodi said, and hugged me.

"Tired already?"

"I've been feeling a little sleepy lately," it said, and at my expression added, "It's the heat."

The heat? It wasn't so bad today. I shifted my tail in a shrug. "Of course. Make sure you're awake after sun-down, though!"

"I wouldn't miss it for anything!" Thodi grinned, then clambered down from the perch. I heard its footsteps as it hopped off the bed of the wagon and padded away.

Some time later, I went to bathe and change into something more festive. I didn't have much to choose from, but what I had would not embarrass the caravan. The tarnished silver and brown pebble chain I left around my waist—it was almost as old as I was, and had belonged to my sibling before her contract had been sold. I added a few matching strands of beads to my tail and mane, leaving the latter loose. I hooked a bronze and blue long-cloth at my hips with cord and silver chain, letting the panel of linen fall to my ankles and separating the hind-panel so it fell on either side of my tail.

Outside, the other eperu of Ledin's caravan had gathered near our fire pit, talking, their best jewelry flashing in the orange firelight. Ledin among them all was loveliest: it had been anadi at birth, and then emodo before it had finally Turned eperu, and had kept the best of all the sexes.

"Bright night!" Ledin said, catching my elbows. "It is good to see you in finery."

"You too," I said, pushing aside one of its curls so I could see its face. It had accentuated the spirals on its cheeks with ground malachite. "We will show a good spirit to Batasil."

"Ekanoi!"

I glanced back—one of the eperu, only half-dressed and wearing an expression of great perplexity, stood panting. "What is it?"

"Thodi is asking for you."

It succeeded in passing its confusion to me. Frowning, I said, "It is in my caravan?"

The eperu nodded, and I strode that way. No light illuminated my wagon, and all its sails had been pulled flush to the frame; I could not see inside. I approached from the front, climbing over the driver's bench. "Thodi?"

A tiny whimper answered me, and my ears flattened. Had it hurt itself? I took the lantern down from beside the bench and lit the wick, then slid into the wagon and held the light up.

Thodi was sitting on my trunk, knees curled to its chest, hugging itself and trembling. It showed no obvious signs of illness, and I stepped closer. "Ba Thodi?"

"Ekanoi," Thodi whispered, and unfolded.

And I saw them... the tiny points of its—her breasts.

I sucked in a breath and hung the lantern from a hook on the ceiling frame. Sitting beside her, I said, "Oh, Thodi."

"Does this mean . . . I'm going to be anadi?" she asked, chin trembling.

"Ssh, don't weep," I said, touching her jaw. "Thodi . . . I'm sorry. It means you already are anadi. Your body is just changing to fit that now."

"But I don't want to be female!" Thodi reached for my waist. "What will I do?"

"What all females do," I said, ears splaying. "You'll go to a good House, be pampered, fed choice foods, rest on pillows by cool pools of water—"

"And have babies until my mind dies and I get as stupid as a soup-beast!" Thodi wailed and began sobbing, nose wrinkling back from fangs that wept acrid tears.

I embraced her, trying not to cringe. "That doesn't happen to all anadi. . . ."

"Just most of them! Ekanoi, please . . . take me with you! I don't want to go to a House and be a pampered anadi breeder. I want to trade, and explore and travel. I want to see new places! I want . . . I want to be eperu, not anadi!"

"You can't argue with your body, Thodi," I said. Gently I disengaged her arms and held her away from me. "You are anadi now. And as much as I want to, we can't take you with us. You'll die out there. Breeders are too fragile for traveling. That's why only eperu trade."

Yellow tears streaked Thodi's lower chin. "Wh-what now?"

What indeed. I sighed and wiped the tears away with my thumbs. "Now . . . we talk to Ledin. It will know what to do."

Ledin looked once at Thodi, then said, "My wagon."

We followed it, sat inside as it pulled all the sails to the frame and then entered, sitting on the trunk across from us.

"This was not in our plan," I said, mouth quirking wryly.

Ledin chuckled. "No, it wasn't." It reached for Thodi's hands and squeezed them. "This is your second Turning, isn't it?"

Thodi nodded, despondent. Her mane fell in tumbled curls over her shoulders, hiding the evidence of her coming change.

"I told her we couldn't take her with us," I said.

Ledin shook its head, paint on its cheeks a-glitter. "No. We don't know what's out there. Even if we did, half a year's journey would be too hard on an anadi." It paused. "We will have to get you someplace you will be safe."

"I don't want to be safe," Thodi said. "I want to be happy."

"I'm sorry." Ledin's voice softened. "I cannot be responsible for you on such a trip. You would sicken, Thodi."

"How do you know?" Thodi asked, ears flattening, voice almost a snarl. "No one ever lets the anadi out to see how long they last!"

Ledin leaned back. "I was anadi for a while."

A white flush clouded Thodi's ears and she looked away.

I touched her shoulder. "We only want to do what's best for you. Letting you die is not part of that."

Her small shoulders slumped. "What will you do with me?"

Ledin sighed. "I suppose I will ask Batasil to take you on its return circuit. Ask it to broker your contract for us, make sure you are released into an honorable and prosperous House. A place they'll take good care of you."

"If anyone can find you a good place to live, it's Batasil," I added.

Thodi let out a long breath. "I guess I don't have a choice," she said.

Ledin shook its head, and I remained silent.

"Sell me, then," she said with a tremor in her voice, and walked out of the wagon.

I rose to follow her, but Ledin's hand on my arm stayed me.

"Let her go. Her weepiness might be anadi frailty or just shock, but she's been raised eperu. Let her have dignity."

"Dignity for freedom—I call that a poor trade, Ledin," I said, ears sloping back.

"I know," Ledin said. "We'll do all we can to provide for her." It stood. "Come with me to talk to Batasil?"

I hesitated, then flicked my tail in a shrug. What else could I do for Thodi?

So as our eperu mingled in the purple shadows and yellow light of Batasil's caravan circle, Ledin and I sat in the lead wagon with cups of steaming tea. Batasil had insisted on pulling out great armfuls of plush pillows for our rumps, draping us with expensive silks "against the wind," bringing out the nicest set of pottery it owned for our use. All so obviously out of its desire to share its wealth with us that I just couldn't be angry . . . or even jealous.

"Now, you wanted to ask me something?" Batasil said, sitting across from us in the nest of pillows and silks. The incredible lace veil it wore pinned behind its ears draped over its shoulders as it leaned toward us.

Ledin put the tea cup aside and rested its hands on its knees. "A few towns back we picked up an orphan, ke Batasil. It Turned today."

"Let me guess," Batasil said. "Anadi."

Ledin nodded, and Batasil's ears drooped. "I'd hoped to be wrong...."

"But you knew we would hardly be coming to you about a Turning eperu," Ledin said. "And had it Turned emodo, we would have left it here to await our return, and escorted it to a better town ourselves. But an anadi... " Ledin shook its head. "We can't wait. She needs a place now. We were hoping you could take her back with you, make sure she was traded into a good House."

"You cannot do this yourselves?" Batasil looked surprised. "You would trust me to do this?"

"We are heading to the northwest," Ledin said.

"What's northwest?"

"We don't know. That's why we're going."

Batasil blinked a few times, then laughed. "Oh, ke Ledin. You were always a risk-taker. Living on the edge of profitability. I think you like to be hungry!"

"We are eperu, ke Batasil. We can go hungry. Thodi cannot." Ledin tapped its knees nervously. "We will not be back this way for half a year. Will you take her for us? Please, ke eperu."

"Of course!" Batasil seemed surprised. "Do you even have to ask? I could no more leave an anadi to privation than I could allow a baby to suffer. I will make sure she is taken care of."

"Thank you," Ledin said, letting out a breath.

Batasil shook its head. "Nothing. It is nothing. Now go, enjoy my food and wine. Leave your troubles for the evening, and bring me the female tomorrow before you go."

We left the wagon, but neither of us had the spirit for a party. The Trinity had made the eperu so that we needed no true sleep . . . but I wished for that brief oblivion that evening, if only to keep from wondering what would have happened had I become anadi on my final Turning at second puberty. Would I have comported myself as well as Thodi?

I counted stars, and thought not.

In the morning, we escorted a sullen Thodi to Batasil's caravan. Batasil stood waiting for us, more conservatively attired in only half the jewelry it had been wearing the evening before, the long-cloth at its hips a gauzy thing of lace and beads and gossamer. I did not doubt that this wealthy eperu, so accustomed to traveling through high circles, could find Thodi a home where she might sleep in a pile of shell if she so desired.

As Ledin and Batasil talked, I turned to Thodi. "Why don't you leave us messages?" I asked.

"Messages?" Thodi said. She held her arms crossed at her chest.

"You know our trade route. If you want, you can have a courier keep news of you for us at one of the het."

"Would that make you feel better?" Thodi asked, and I couldn't decide whether she was bitter or honestly inquiring.

"I would like to hear from you," I said. My ears canted back. "I will miss you, ba Thodi."

"Ke Thodi, now," she said. "I am an adult." She lifted her chin.

"Goodbye, Ekanoi."

She turned from me and strode away, head still high.

I sought some sign that Thodi did not blame us for our actions, but she never looked back at me. When I swallowed, I was surprised to taste bitter tears. Furtively, I licked my fangs clean and waited for Ledin to finish talking with Batasil.

Ledin and I walked to our wagons, where the eperu were harnessing the beasts and making preparations for our grand venture.

"I'm sorry, Ekanoi."

I glanced at Ledin. "It's not your fault."

"I know. But I grieve with you anyway. The life of an anadi is difficult to accept when you have been anything else. Even emodo have more freedom."

I resisted the urge to look over my shoulder. "Did . . . did we do the right thing?"

"We did the necessary thing." Ledin's mouth nearly made a smile. "Whether that's right or not . . . I don't know."

It left me for its wagon, and I went to mine: empty now of all of Thodi's things. I sat on the driver's bench and pressed my hand to my mouth to keep from weeping.

But the beasts wanted harnessing, and I still needed to snap the sails back to make shade against the morning sun. I did my chores and fell into line behind Ledin's wagon as we made our way out of Het Ikoped and into the unknown.

Het Ikoped presented the same face to us when we unhitched our wagons there in the early spring, but I saw something different in it anyway. I saw how small it was, this collection of brick and stone houses erected against a vast sky. I saw the broken road leading southeast from its edge as a paved walkway to civilization, and Jokka, and places crowded with the familiar.

I saw that we had changed, and the world had not, and that was good.

No exotic goods clustered our wagons. On our journey we'd discovered rocks and thin slopes, and on the horizon autumn copper and scarlet suggesting hills, perhaps even a forest. We hadn't reached it before we ran out of supplies. We'd skinned the animals we'd eaten and saved their pelts, and we'd collected a few bundles of shiny rocks—nothing stunningly valuable, save to the eperu who'd seen their origins.

We would have done it again, even knowing we would have so little at its end.

I finished watering my pack animals and jogged to Ledin's wagon.

"Well," it said, standing on the bench and breathing in the familiar air. "Shall we see what grain prices are like today?"

I laughed. "We should be trying to purchase useful cargo, Ledin. Not spending shell on dreams. It's time for prudence."

Ledin sighed. "Prudence. What fun."

"No, but necessary."

It hopped down beside me. "Let's go find a drink before we turn entirely to prudence, friend."

I glanced around Het Ikoped again, thought of how small it was, and shook my head. "So tiny. Maybe a drink will make it seem big again."

"Unlikely, but worth trying."

I chuckled.

We walked toward the wayfarer's house, talking quietly, intent only on ourselves—probably why the male almost knocked us over.

"Pardon me!" he said. "You are with the caravan, ke Ledin's caravan?"

We glanced at one another. Ledin said, "I'm Ledin. May I help you, ke emodo?"

"Ah, yes. I have been waiting to discharge a message to your caravan's members." He opened a bag and withdrew a large package. "This is yours. Will you mark my token?"

Ledin rummaged in its pouch, and the two went through the transaction process.

"Thank you. Be well!"

We watched him go, and Ledin handed me the package: soft leather, dyed a dark blue. "What do you suppose?"

"I don't know," Ledin said. "But let's go gather the others and find out."

Ten minutes later, the eperu of the caravan crowded around our fire pit as Ledin opened the package. It withdrew a piece of parchment, bleached pale, so fabulously expensive as to draw gasps of astonishment from the others. Then three stone boxes, each three hands tall.

Ledin's eyes widened. "Void and Brightness," it whispered.

I looked. The paper's surface gleamed, colored chalks fixed with a layer of gum. The vibrant rendering depicted an anadi . . . Thodi, her skin gleaming with soft tans and lavender, dark hair mussed over her face. She stood with her hips thrust back and her chest forward, one arm lifted above her head, and she was beautiful.

Ledin traced the words beneath the image, and read aloud for the eperu of the caravan who could not. "To Ledin and Ekanoi and all the eperu of the caravan. I told Batasil to give you everything. Please bring back something pretty from the wild for me. Thodi Pazaña-eperu, Het Makali."

Ledin opened the first box and almost dropped it. I grabbed Ledin's wrists to steady them, for I'd seen the gleam of the box's contents. Shells, hundreds of them, each as large as my thumb. The second box held the same.

"Trinity!" one of the eperu said, holding the second box reverently. "How much money must Batasil have charged for Thodi's contract?"

"Whatever it was, it must have been astronomical for this to be left after Batasil's commission," Ledin said.

"And she left it all to us," I said softly.

Ledin gingerly set the first box on the ground and opened the final box. In it another piece of parchment rested atop a set of gleaming jewels. The parchment read: "This is for Ekanoi."

I withdrew the gems and found in my hands a heavy waist-chain of bright silver, cabochon sapphire, and pearl. It had two clasps, meant to be hooked to an anadi kaña's navel ring . . . and surely only a kaña, the Jokkad deemed most valuable in a House, could afford such a thing. Somehow I doubted the silver would tarnish.

Ledin said quietly, "This is more than enough shell to return to the northwest. Enough shell to buy supplies for several years."

"Do we want to spend it all?" one of the others said.

Ledin lifted one of the spiral shells, flawless cream and coral-pink. "We wouldn't have to." It looked up. "Are we ready to go back?"

As with the first time, it needn't have asked.

I stood as they talked of the faraway forest and its riches, walked away to sit on the bench of my wagon. I set the heavy chain in my lap and caressed it. As I stared at its elegance, contemplated its weight, Ledin came by. It met my eyes, then handed me the parchment with the drawing and left.

I studied the rendering, touched its shining surface with my fingertips. Thodi smiled back at me, mischievous, a little sultry. Not happy, perhaps . . . but content. In her navel she had a ring, heavier than the one we would have put on her ear had she remained with us. Remained eperu.

My sibling's waist chain I stored in my trunk, with my other finery. Around my hips I draped instead a fortune's worth of female jewels. And then I went to do my chores and join the celebration by the fire.

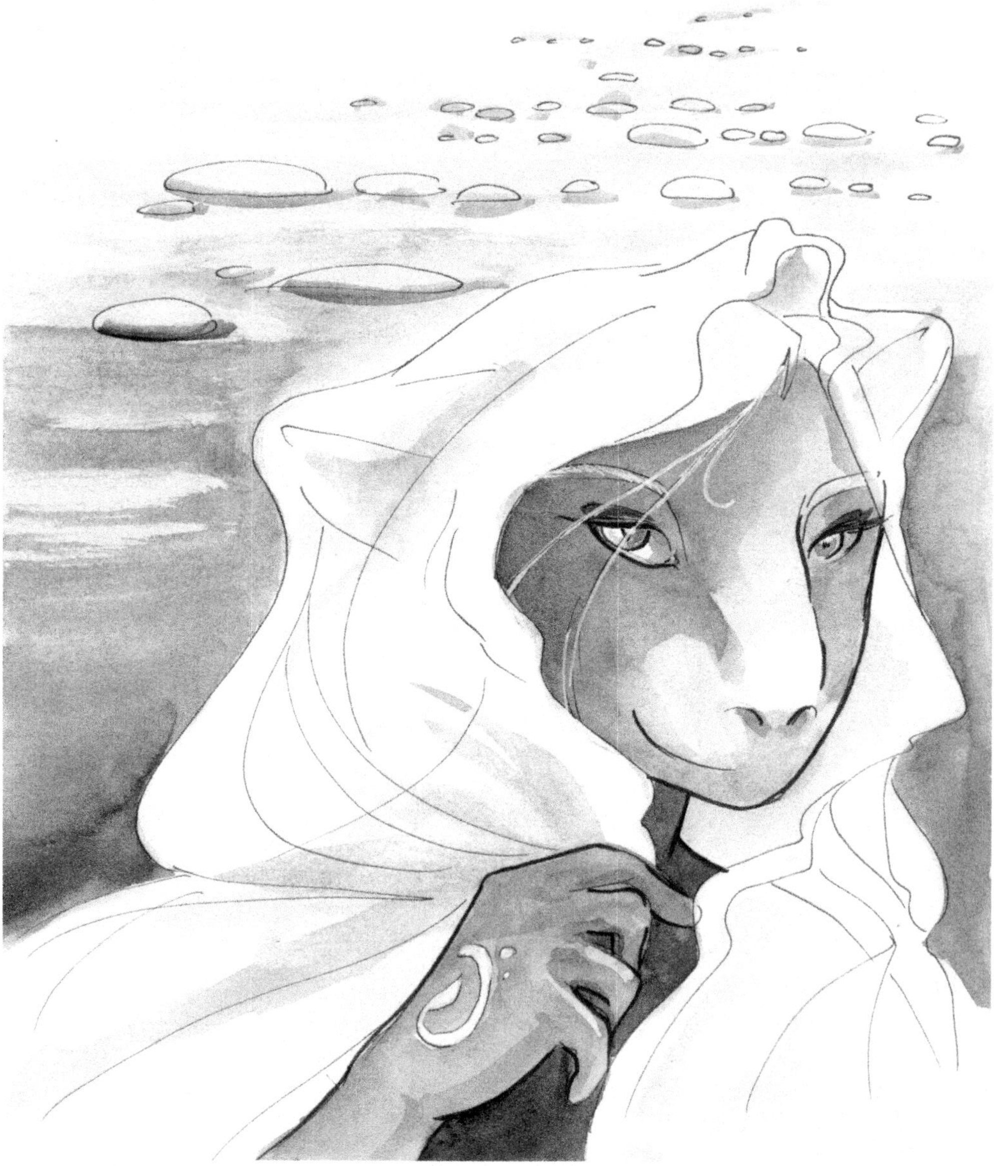

Unspeakable

"I'M NOT SURE THIS is a good idea," I said to Nashada as he pulled me toward the knot of silhouettes gathered near the ruins. "Can't we go home and play jenadha, or find someplace to have tea?"

"We've played jenadha a thousand times beneath these stars, setasha," Nashada said to me. He was far freer with sweet names than I was. "We've drunk so much tea I might weep it next time I cry. I want to do something different. Besides, I've already paid our entrance to the clay. Don't you trust me?"

I eyed my lover warily. After a long day shaping metal and glass beads into dangles, I would have been content to relax outside beneath the trees. Nashada, on the other hand, conducted hunts through the ruins, drank late at night at different cheldzan, and attended parties and clays at any hour he could contrive. I loved him, tail to ear-tip, but trusting him to choose my entertainment was a different matter.

"Oh, come on," Nashada said, pulling me after him.

Beneath crumbled blocks and behind partial walls, deep

shadows hid from the light cast by fire bowls. The Jokka waiting with us for admission to the clay were washed in the numinous palette, gold glimmering, purple darkness. I knew I would recognize no one in the morning, and while I could appreciate the artistry, it heightened my discomfort.

"Why is it so dark?"

"It's supposed to be mysterious," Nashada said, grinning. "It's a special clay."

My misgivings doubled. "What do you mean, 'special'?"

"This clay-keeper, everyone calls her Ke Pediná. She writes naughty stories."

Before I could voice the objections that crowded my throat, Nashada dragged me in, handing two claim stones to the eperu at the arch. The seating area was no more than a selection of broken stone benches and fallen columns, artfully draped with veils.

"Naughty stories?" I hissed at Nashada once he'd chosen us a bench. "What are you talking about?"

Nashada's slender fangs shone in his smile. "What more do you need to know? Ke Pediná sets down graphic love stories. I thought it might be fun to come and see just how graphic they were."

My mouth worked, but I had no words. Clay-keepers were among the most honored members of our society, for they guarded our history, our stories, our knowledge. Periodically, they set out pieces of our truths with their collections of painted stones and clay bits: stories spelled out, letter by letter, for people to read. The thought that one of Het Kabbanil's clay-keepers used his precious store of letters to set out graphic love stories explained why he needed a title to hide behind... and Ke Pediná, "Honored Tease," only stressed the indecency of the idea.

Then Nashada's choice of pronoun finally registered. My voice rose in horror. "'Her'? The clay-keeper is an anadi?"

"Hush!" Nashada said. He glanced around to ensure we'd disturbed no one before continuing. "I don't know. No one knows. I just choose to think of her as anadi because that would be even more outrageous. Don't you think? An anadi writing graphic love stories?"

I groaned and hid my face in his shoulder. "Nashada!"

He stroked my mane back from my cheek. I could hear the grin in his voice. "There, there, Tañel. We'll cure you of your modesty."

The rustle of feet and whisper of voices stilled behind me, and I lifted my head. Several of the veils fell away, hissing against the stone. Only one gossamer cloth separated us from the clay area, and behind its mist a Jokkad moved.

Illuminated only by the fire, her figure shrouded in diaphanous clothes, she drifted in a nimbus of copper light. I thought of a star come to the World, but the light was too furtive ... too private. I was immediately taken by her grace, the sweep of the thin cloth as it trailed her body.

Entranced, we watched in silence, the audience united by our reaction to her beauty. She set down the stones of her story one by one, moving in and out of the twilight's blue shadows.

It wasn't until the thin curtain rippled to the ground before us that I realized she hadn't reappeared from the last shadow that had swallowed her. I shook my head, trying to remember where I was. At the clays I'd attended before, the story had always been prepared ahead of time. No one had incorporated their arrangement into a performance like this.

One by one the audience crossed the divide into the viewing area, Nashada and I among them. Hundreds of stones the size of my fist, each painted with a letter, were lined up in a rectangle on swept earth. The clay-keeper had chosen the snake form: there was enough space between each sentence and the next for the readers to walk, and at the end of the line one reversed direction and walked the opposite way to read the next line. The snake form was a favorite for fiction, since reading backwards heightened the suspense.

I read. And I blushed white at the ears and cheeks, until I thought all the blood in my head would make it too heavy for my body to carry. "Graphic" didn't begin to describe the story, a tale about two emodo discovering their new love—lust—for one another, discovering and sating themselves. Some words were so frequently used they merited their own stones. I glanced at the other readers. There were eperu, neuters, here. How many of them had been emodo—male—before Turning? Was it titillating for those who'd never been emodo to know how males consummated their relationships?

I left halfway through the story, exiting at the end of a line and trotting through the arch into the unlit ruins. Nashada didn't call after me—it would have been impolite to disturb the others—but I knew he would look for me later. I tried to get lost, ducking beneath several columns and hiding at last in the shadow of a fallen doorway.

I had crouched there long enough to regain my composure when the light of the stars glided over a figure in gossamer. My breath caught in my mouth.

When the shadows released the last of the figure, I found myself staring into the solemn face of an eperu dressed in pants, long-cloth, and a diaphanous mantle. It held the cloth closed at its throat.

"You're her? Ke Pediná?" I exclaimed.

It grinned. "I won't tell if you don't."

"Okay," I said, still too shocked to think.

It offered me a hand and its name. "Ekkuli Molan-emodo."

"Molan-emodo?" I glanced at its feet, sought and found the evidence that it had been born male in the elegance of its feet-hands . . . but that did not explain the delicacy of its shoulders, the slim fangs, whispers of a female shape it did not wear.

Without prompting, it knew what I wanted to know, or perhaps I hadn't been subtle enough in my examination. "I'm ethilik."

Elithik—every-sexed, we would say. So Ekkuli had been born emodo, Turned anadi at first puberty, and finally settled at eperu, the sex it would remain for the balance of its life. "I . . . I'm not sure what to say," I said.

"Tell me your name?" Ekkuli said.

"Tañel. Tañel Ithera-emodo." I came out from under the doorway, my footsteps uncertain.

"You left early," Ekkuli said. "You didn't like my story?"

"It was . . ." I warred with myself. What could I say? Obscene? Not to my taste? Different? Well-written? It had been all those things. I realized that the eperu was watching my struggle with amusement and chose honesty. "No. I don't know."

"Ah," Ekkuli said. "Rare that, and appreciated. A clay-keeper rarely hears truth, even though truth is our deepest calling."

"You call that truth?" I asked.

Ekkuli grinned. "Was it not accurate?"

I blushed and looked away.

"Was it not tender? Did it not touch off ripples in your heart?" A pause. "You needn't answer, ke emodo. But I suspect you know something of what I speak. I saw your companion . . . he was more than a friend."

"You saw me leave, you saw me come in . . . were you watching me in particular?" I asked, unnerved.

It shook its head. "No. No more than I watch everything. It is part of my work . . . observing how things are."

I snorted. "And that's how you find your truths, ah?"

"Yes." Ekkuli grinned.

I shook my head. "Anyone could find truth that way."

"Ah! But would they be brave enough to set it down?"

I wrinkled my nose. "There's a difference between bravery and brazenness."

Ekkuli laughed then, and startled me by it, for its laugh was low and intimate. I felt as if it had shone a light into its soul for my eyes.

"You cut me, ke emodo. Will you give me another chance to tell you a truth? Perhaps one you will think less brazenly graphic?"

I was intrigued despite my better judgement. "Maybe."

"If 'maybe' becomes 'yes,' return in a few hours and read what I set out. Maybe then you will change your mind." One tufted ear flicked outward, just visible beneath the mantle. "Your lover seeks you. I'll leave him to you."

"I—"

But Ekkuli was gone, and there was Nashada tramping through the dust and rubble of the ruins. "Setasha! You left just before the best part! And now they're closing the whole thing and you won't be able to read the rest."

I turned to him, strangely reticent to mention Ekkuli's visit. "I'm sorry, Nashada. I know you paid for me. Maybe you can tell me the rest?"

"Not with the same flair as Ke Pediná! But since you asked so nicely...."

I left Nashada wearing a smile in his sleep and crept through the silent halls until I found a little-used ramp to the top. Het Kabbanil was our largest city, or so I'd heard from the caravan traders who stop here. Hundreds of buildings of baked clay huddled in the shadows of the extensive stone sites left from some distant age. Some Houses built their steadings among those ruins, incorporating some of the remaining walls and floors.

My House, Ithera, was more sensible. Of the ancient sites that comprised old Het Kabbanil we had chosen to live where our ancestors had dug: a selection of rooms hollowed out of the earth, where the cool air was kind to our anadi and kept our food from spoiling quickly. I loved the solitude and the temperature, but sneaking out of Ithera would have been easier had our windows been on the walls instead of the ceilings.

Once I slid outside, a chill took me. It was later than I'd imagined, close enough to truedark to make me think twice about Ekkuli's offer. I could make it there before the black wiped the World from my sight, but how would I read the story?

I ran, trusting the evening's cool to keep me safe. Every emodo has to carefully experiment to determine his physical limits; beyond that, danger waits, the same mind-death that hunts the anadi but with less success. I had never experienced the dizziness that warned of a mind-wound, but I didn't want this to be the first time. Thus I wasn't surprised when truedark swept toward me even as I stumbled into the ruins.

No Jokkad travels during truedark. Breeders sleep through this dangerous hour; eperu doze-dream in it, weaving nightmarish visions from the absolute black. We are a people of great clarity of sight, and to lose that facility is powerfully affecting. I froze on the edge of the ruins, unsure of my footing, unsure even of the World beneath my feet. I flexed my toes, fighting panic.

A shimmer of light streamed past me, and then another. I recognized the firebrights from stories—an insect attracted by the honey of the black yew tree's flowers. A knot of them tangled a little ways before me, and their glow gave just enough light for me to crawl forward. I barked my knees and shins several times on the way, but before long I found myself standing at the viewing area.

Three large rocks had been arranged in a triangle, each smeared with sap. The firebrights dancing above them gave more than enough light to see the story set between the stones. This one had been arranged in a stanza form with baked clay letters not even as long as my smallest claw. I had to kneel and lean onto my hands to read them.

It was a very short tale, in three stanzas.

An eperu, a dancer, with flashing eye,
like bright stars and
sweet truedark-honey,
Each step a song, each gesture a joy.
Lucky in love, luckily loved
by an eperu in dusk—

Turned anadi, the last choice,
Nature's irony and
lover's dismay. But the House
thought to keep her, to breed her.
Dusk's eperu did too.
Their love sweet between them—

And sticky—and long—and gentle,
A love without names, without
rules. No one knew.
No one asked. No one learned.
They loved until mind-death
took her away: sweet setasha.

I reared back, shuddering, and pressed my hand to my mouth. For fear of what, I wasn't sure: that I would scream, or weep, or tear out my own wrists . . . to keep my hands from sweeping the abomination away.

I stumbled away into the utter dark, and regarded not at all the bruises I collected on my way home.

I woke before Nashada and went to my bath, fighting nausea. I had already dressed and was braiding dangles into my hair when Nashada propped himself up. His yawn displayed needle-sharp fangs, a maneuver he'd perfected when he discovered how attractive I found them.

"You're up early," he said. "It's not even time for work yet."

"I just wanted to meet the day," I said. I didn't want to tell Nashada about the errand I was planning, the one I'd been mulling while I tossed and turned the remainder of the night.

"Before the field-workers?" His tone of voice held notes of skepticism and affection. A few moments later, he joined me at the table and looped his arms around my waist from behind. "You're not a great fan of the dawning hour, setasha. Are you sure there's not something I can help you with?"

For the briefest of instants, I considered it, considered sharing the depth of my shame, my outrage, my horror with him. But even wild Nashada would shun me for the truth I hid in my heart, even if I could force myself to repeat Ekkuli's appalling story. I said nothing, bowing my head.

"If that's how you want it," Nashada said. He nuzzled the top of my head before pulling away. "I'll see you at break?"

"Of course," I said.

Nashada left for the bathing chambers, and I rested my hands on the table. He loved me so much, and so freely.

With a sigh, I let myself out of the house and headed for the major thoroughfare through Het Kabbanil. I was a jeweler, a position that did not require me to wake with the sun like Nashada's did—he was a beast-master who sold his services to the farming Houses—but my elders became uncomfortable if I did not begin my work by the third hour after dawn. I had to complete my errand by then.

Half an hour later I found myself in the town proper. I had to ask a few passersby after my destination, and I needed the greater part of an hour to find it.

I spared a moment's gladness for the finery I'd donned, for House Molan was more prosperous than I'd expected. They'd cleaned and retouched the remaining ruins of their chosen site, and had used the freestanding columns and unexpected walls as accent pieces around the buildings they'd constructed for their families. Crawling vines with large cream blossoms curled in almost skin-like patterns across the modern buildings, certainly maintained by a skilled staff. I had no sooner passed through the stone arch when an eperu dressed in elegant vest, long-cloths, and pants appeared from behind a column.

"May I help you, ke emodo?" it asked.

"I've come to speak with the Head of House Molan."

The eperu canted its head. "On what matter?"

"It is about the activities of one of your members," I said.

The eperu gestured assent. "If you will follow me? The Head may not be free, but one of his auxiliaries should be available."

"My thanks," I said, and followed. I trembled as I walked, the disgust rising again. I could taste it, sour and hot, on the back of my throat. With it came fear . . . fear for myself, fear for others. Stories can be dangerous. What if I was not the only Jokkad Ekkuli had subjected to its truedark tales?

The eperu showed me to a fine room in one of the larger buildings. I sat on a bench shrouded in soft pillows, unaware of time's passage as I stared out the window, mesmerized by the droop and sway of the blossoms in the breeze.

The male who entered surprised me thus. I jerked upright.

"My pardon!" I exclaimed, rising, horrified that he'd found me half-asleep.

The emodo touched his head in the male's greeting. I returned it as I struggled to take him in, for his piercing regard trapped my eyes to his. He had beast eyes, yellow-green . . . but where most hide such eyes, aware of their ugliness, he used them to intimidate. I could find no emotion in his predator's gaze.

"May I help you?" he asked, and the curtness of the words implied how little help he felt obliged to give.

"I came . . . about one of your House," I said.

"Yes?"

"An eperu," I said, gathering my convictions. I remembered my outrage at the sight of the story, my disgust, my horror. "Ekkuli. Your clay-keeper. It is writing unusual stories—"

"Something other than its sexual stories?" the emodo asked.

"You know?" I asked, barely suppressing my surprise.

"Of course," he said. "Ekkuli's stories bring us a great deal of shell. More than it would have had it been a traditional clay-keeper. Did its stories offend unduly?"

"They're not just sexual stories," I said, thinking of the horrible poem. Trying not to think about love across genders. "Love stories. Unseemly ones."

The faintest of frowns creased the emodo's brow. His unwavering stare grew cold and intense, but no longer focused. I imagined him seeking Ekkuli's image in his mind and directing that spear-point regard on the eperu, and suddenly dismay clouded out the disgust in my heart.

"You are not the first to say this," he said. "Unseemly in what way?"

"As all love stories are," I said, mentally backpedaling. "Private matters are no fit subject for a clay reading."

He focused again on me, and though his eyes had lost their sharpness my unease remained. "Ah, I see. I apologize for your poor experience. Your shell will be refunded and someone will speak with Ekkuli."

"That's not really necessary," I began.

"You were distressed. It is not our business to distress those who pay us," the emodo interrupted. "Your escort will return shortly with your money. Good day."

I did not have time to reply before he left. As he'd promised, the eperu who'd led me in returned with a soft bag full of shells. It handed the bag over and led me out.

Shame makes a poor companion. I accomplished little work that day, none of it inspired. I retired early and slept until evening, and deeply at that. When I woke, Nashada's dirty clothing had been tossed into the corner basket and his jewels were gone. Somehow I'd slept through his return, his typically noisy preparations for the evening and his departure. I looked into his stone bowl and found a red ball of clay: he had gone to the cheldzan beside the stream, for tea; I was welcome to come or not as I desired.

Paper is very expensive, even in Het Kabbanil. Most Jokka use stone tablets or wooden plates treated with wax so they can be wiped and re-used. Nashada and I use bowls: a blue-gray one for him, after his skin tone, and a darker gray one for me. We tell one another where we are and whether we want company with different tokens.

I did not go. I did not want to see other Jokka. My unease about having gone to House Molan had only heightened with the passing day. What Jokkad walked abroad at truedark, anyway? Who would see the story? Who could it harm?

Why had Ekkuli done it?

Why did I feel that trouble already hunted Ke Pediná?

My evening walk took me to the clay-keeper's ruins, but I did not pay to read the story. I sat outside and waited, and after the last of the audience had dispersed Ekkuli came out to meet me. Still shrouded in its mantle, it sat beside me, so close I could feel the edges of the cloth tickling my bare arm.

"Did you glimpse the braided tail of truth then, ke emodo?" it asked.

My ears flattened. "There are truths that are best kept hidden. Thoughts that should remain edloña, unspoken, unthought," I said. I handed it the bag of shell House Molan had returned me.

"Ah, no! Such a wound, that a word even exists for that which should not be said! Ke emodo, there are no truths so shabby, vile, or perilous that they don't merit the gaze of a Jokkad." It took the bag, and I noticed the delicacy of its fingers, a stark reminder of its birth sex. Usually only emodo have such nimble hands. "What's this?" it asked.

Had Molan not reprimanded it? Had my ill-considered visit wreaked no damage—no further damage? The relief that flooded me at the thought startled. I cared, then, for this speaker of unspeakable truths.

"It belongs to you," I said of the pouch.

"You confuse me," Ekkuli said, though it sounded intrigued. "You tell me there are truths that need hiding, and yet you give me shell . . . as compensation for the story?"

"Perhaps I am the one who's confused," I said. "But keep the shell."

Its fingers massaged the bag. "This is more than wonted. Payment for more than one story. Perhaps I should set out another for you later."

"Perhaps you should," I said, before I knew what I said. "Or perhaps you shouldn't. To speak edloña is dangerous."

Ekkuli laughed again, that delightful, low, intimate sound. "So it is, ke emodo."

"Tañel," I interrupted.

It grinned at me. "Tañel, then. The risks are worth taking, to find those who will meet your heart halfway. Come tonight, if it pleases you, and see how little the word *edloña* means to a true clay-keeper."

I came back that night and read about an anadi who lived a long and wondrous life, having borne many children and never lost her intelligence to the mind-death that preys so readily on females. I wept at the end of that one, licking tears from my fangs at the thought of a mother who could still speak with her children after they'd become adults. Who would have thought of such a thing? Only Ekkuli, fearless Ekkuli.

The eperu signed that one with a single *e*, a hooked and dotted loop with an extra claw-dot; a joke it shared with me, for on the rare occasions someone was found edloña, they were marked with such a letter before they were cast out. I ran my finger over the extra mark, shivering at the passage from rough stone to slick paint. I picked up the rock and tucked it in my pocket, reacting to the sense of unease that had plagued me all day. I had no shell with me to compensate for the stone, so I pulled one of the rings off a foot-finger and left it there. The night engulfed its brass sheen.

I returned every night that followed. Ekkuli and I did not have to meet; the eperu set out a new truedark truth, assuming I would arrive. We evolved our own method of communication. A story that touched me would be rewarded by shells or smaller semi-precious stones. I stole the signatures from stories that disquieted me. Over time, the eperu began to answer some of my more oblique or enigmatic responses with stories that addressed them. It also played with its signature, putting out the double-marked *e* only when it thought a story would particularly perturb me, as if daring me to steal the stone. Sometimes I did. Sometimes I didn't.

I read them all, and dreamed, and shivered in my blankets beside Nashada's warm body. None of them were comfortable tales, and most of them were edloña, unspeakable, unthinkable. Why I returned, I could not say.

One night, I entered my room and turned to the bed to find Nashada leaning on an elbow, watching me in the dark. I stopped moving, my breath caught in my throat.

"Did you think I wasn't noticing?" he asked softly.

"I had hoped," I started, then realized the futility of it. I sat on the edge of the bed and sighed.

"If you've found another, you can tell me," Nashada said. "I want you to be happy."

"It's not that!" I exclaimed, then lowered my voice, conscious of the darkness pressing in above us. Truedark is not only the time of fantasies, but also of confidences; even so, it was hard to begin. "It's the clay-keeper you took me to. I've been reading stories by it."

"This late?" Nashada canted his head.

"It sets out special ones after everyone else goes home. For me." I bowed my head, unwilling to show off the white blush that stained my cheeks and ears. I might as well have been spending time with another male. "It's a complicated story."

"I see!" Nashada said, and incredibly he laughed. "So Ke Pediná is an eperu, and you are taken with it! I knew you would like the clay-keeper more than you were willing."

"It's not that!" I said. "It doesn't set out love stories for me, not the kind that we saw. They're . . . they're different."

"Different how?" Nashada asked, cheerful.

"They're edloña," I said, and held my breath. I hadn't realized how much I trusted Nashada until this moment, and then—

"No wonder it puts them out late at night," Nashada mused. "I would do the same, were I the clay-keeper. Are they good?"

I looked into his dark green eyes and saw only interest, love, and curiosity. My breath escaped in a shuddering sigh, and Nashada wrapped his arms around my waist.

"It's that hard for you, isn't it," he murmured. "But still, you try. I am proud of you, setasha."

I leaned into his arms, relieved.

"But it's not particularly safe for you to be seen leaving the House every night. It's too unusual. Someone might wonder what you were doing and follow you."

"But the stories!"

Nashada grinned. "How's this. I'll go out every other night, come back and tell you what it says. Then you do the same for me. And I'll teach you how to be more discreet about your night wandering."

I paused. For an instant, I hated the idea of sharing Ekkuli with anyone, of sharing our code, our communication. But the stories . . . the stories were worth sharing. And Nashada didn't have to know about the system; he could develop his own.

"Okay," I said.

"Why don't you start with tonight's?" Nashada said, pulling me into the blankets and helping me discard my clothing. "A little lulling tale to help us sleep?"

"I doubt it qualifies," I said, but I told him anyway about the House that prospered with an eperu lore-knower as its Head of

Household. Not the stuff of nightmares, but only breeders are allowed to be Heads of Household. Neither of us slept well.

One evening I arrived to find no story between the rocks. Nor did Nashada find one the next night.

"It's not giving its regular clays either," Nashada said the third night, tossing his vest into the basket. He sat on the bed and looked up at me. "Something's wrong."

I nodded, hugging myself. My unease had fledged into true worry. "Maybe this is my fault."

He frowned. "How so?"

Truth is a weed. Once it has its roots in you, it is difficult to ignore. "I went to House Molan about Ekkuli the night after you took me to see it."

"What did you tell them?" Nashada asked. His voice remained even, but I could see the sudden tension that gripped his body.

"I wasn't specific . . . but perhaps it was enough to give them cause to investigate. They made it sound like they'd heard disquieting things about Ekkuli before."

He considered, then gestured his rejection of the idea. "I'd say it was unlikely—you went weeks ago, didn't you?—save for the thought that you might not have been the only one. Still, we shouldn't assume the worst. Maybe it has fallen ill."

"I'll ask in the morning," I said. "I've been to Molan before, I can go again. I might even be able to make up for my complaint by saying something complimentary."

I could not sleep that night, and envied Nashada's easy

drop into dreams; he was working earlier now that the season had advanced. In lieu of pretending to rest, I removed myself to my work room and returned to the piece I'd been working on. I'd taken the ancient symbols for eperu, anadi, and emodo and worked them into a single silver medallion, a circle pierced from below with a mark, sprouting another above, and with a single dot in the middle. I wondered who would buy it, given its meaning. I wondered why I'd made it.

My head drooped toward my work table until it rested among the metal shavings and thin blades. I had never suspected until my great error that I harbored the seeds of horror in my heart. Since then I'd struggled to bury them too deeply to ever sprout.

Ekkuli . . . Ekkuli was sunlight. Its stories were water for my parched spirit. My danger had never been more acute than here, this moment, when the thought of living without Ke Pedinás edloña stories left me weak in the grip of despair. Were I wise, were I enamored with my life as a good Jokkad, a productive member of House Ithera and a respectable craftsman in Het Kabbanil . . . were I wise and good, I would call Ekkuli's disappearance a windfall and leave it be.

I knew I wouldn't. Truth is an impertinent plant.

I approached House Molan with trepidation. It looked no different than it had a few weeks past, but something had changed. Something in me. I stood outside its arch, ignoring the sun's brilliant regard. I had not yet prepared myself to enter when the eperu door-warden appeared.

"May I help you, ke emodo?" it asked politely.

"I'd like to ask after one of your members," I said.

Its ears flattened. "My apologies, ke emodo, but most of House Molan is in Trial."

I stiffened. "I . . . see," I said. "Is it a public matter?"

"The decision will be public if appropriate," the eperu said. "A matter of discipline within the House, you understand. They should be done this evening."

"Of course," I said. "Thank you for your time."

It smiled. "My pleasure is to serve."

I trailed home, my worry become dread. Surely no coincidence saw Ekkuli vanish just before its House sat Trial on one of its members.

When I arrived, Nashada grabbed me and pulled me into our room. "It's all over the field," he said. "They're going to Break Ke Pediná from Molan."

"How can you be sure?" I answered, stricken still with horror. "To exile it just for naughty stories?"

"If they caught it at its truedark tales, they're more than naughty stories, setasha, and you know it well. To speak or perform edloña is more than enough reason to Break a person's contract."

I tried to think through my panic. Breaking someone's contract was more than an escort out of a House . . . it required leaving the city entirely and never returning. A Broken contract was a matter of public record, stored in Transactions to forever haunt its owner. Such a crime is not forgiven among the Jokka. The only reprieve is to flee, and if the sentence is immediate, without more than the clothes on one's body.

With summer approaching, exile was death.

"Was it my fault?" I asked hoarsely.

"What word there is indicates Ekkuli's behavior with us was a pattern. It made a habit of dancing along the edge of what was acceptable," Nashada said. He took a deep breath. "The field-hands could be wrong. Everything may work out as it should."

"Maybe. We'll know this evening," I said.

It was the longest evening of my life. I picked up the tools in my workshop and did not employ them. The tips of my fingers had grown numb; the strength in my hands had drained away. I could only roll one of the tiny stones with its double-dotted *e* in my hands, chafing my palms, chafing my soul.

Nashada joined me a few hours later, resting his hands on my shoulders.

I remained silent a few minutes longer, then said, "I did not take up with you out of desire for you."

"I know."

Ah, but the seed of truth can unfurl in such unexpected ways. I glanced up at him, startled. "You knew?"

"Of course I did," he said. "You never offered your heart and mind to any Jokkad, and I didn't fool myself into thinking I was the special one. It was some other reason, wasn't it."

I nodded, unwilling to say more.

"But you learned to love me, didn't you?"

I stared at the stone cupped in my palm, then smiled and slid my free hand over his. "You are irresistible," I said.

Nashada grinned. "I was counting on it. I wanted to unlock

your mystery myself . . . but I know better now. I needed an eperu's help for that, didn't I."

"It told true stories," I murmured.

"And which one touched your heart so deeply you ran in fear to Molan's doorstep?" Nashada asked, and I was surprised by the gentleness of his voice.

I remained silent, eyes closing. I imagined Ekkuli's presence, a shadow clothed in white gossamer, a creature of demanding contrasts and unyielding sight. "I loved an emodo. Even after he Turned anadi."

Nashada's hands gripped me harder.

"The House kept her, but sold her breeding contract. I loved her until her mind dissolved in the harness. And then I found out why love should remain within sexes." I gulped in a small breath. "To ask someone to love without understanding the risk of being another sex . . . who could encompass it?" I clamped down on my itching fangs, willing the tears back into them. When that didn't work, I resorted to quickly licking my teeth. "And I miss him—her—so much, still. I love her still."

"So you came to Ithera with a broken heart and a fearful mind, thinking someone would know you'd done the unspeakable," Nashada said. He crouched next to me, taking my hands. "And decided for propriety's sake you should take up with an emodo lover immediately, so that no one would question you. Am I right?"

I bowed my head.

"And yet you still allowed yourself to go to Ekkuli. I dare say you love it, even."

"I do not!" I exclaimed, terrified.

Nashada shook his head. "Oh, setasha. Do you see how our society twists us? It only tries to keep us from harm, but in doing so it destroys us. You do love Ekkuli, and why not? It knows your secret heart." He stood, pulling me with him. "Come on."

"Where—where are we going?" I tried to get a hand free to wipe away the tears leaking from my mouth, but Nashada wouldn't release me.

"To go get Ekkuli, of course." He paused. "That's what you want, isn't it?"

I tried to compose myself. "Y-yes. But where will we go? We can't stay in Het Kabbanil."

"No, we can't," Nashada agreed.

"We'll have to go somewhere else," I mused. "Sign with another House."

"Or start a new one," Nashada said cheerfully.

I eyed him.

"We do have the requisites," he said. "At least two people, and one of them a breeder to be Head of Household. We'll even have a clay-keeper, if Ekkuli agrees to go with us."

I stared at him, unable to fathom what motivated that grin. "You want to go with me? Leave the city for the unknown? Help me take up with an eperu?"

"I'm sure Ekkuli won't mind sharing," Nashada said, unperturbed. "And of course I want to go with you. Haven't you noticed that I love you? Now stop gawking and let's go get some rikka. We don't want to leave Ekkuli too long without water."

I followed, bemused.

We found Ekkuli at the last well beyond Het Kabbanil's fields. The eperu had been stripped of its clothes and its diaphanous mantle and in the purple dusk wore only a long-cloth. It was draped over the lip of the well; I could read its despondency from a distance, could shiver with empathy for its slumped shoulders and drooping ears. The eperu did not even lift its head when the clawed toes of our rikka shuffled up to the well's perimeter.

Nashada glanced at me, waiting. I cleared my throat and said, "Ke Ekkuli."

It looked up, eyes wide. I could trace the track of tears across its chin. "Tañel?"

I smiled. "The same. I missed your stories."

Bitterness darkened Ekkuli's eyes. "Well, there will be no more of the stories, I'm afraid."

"So House Molan and Het Kabbanil would have it," I said. "But not I."

Ekkuli's ears splayed and it stared at my rikka's feet. "I'm not sure you understand," it said. "I did it once too often, told the truth one too many times. They've Broken my contract. They sent me away!"

"I know," I said. "You remember Nashada, my companion?"

It lifted its head, confusion plain on its face. "Yes?"

"We thought a great deal of your truth-telling. The other Jokka might not want to hear or read your stories, but we would be honored to have such a brave and powerful clay-keeper in our new House."

"New ... House? You've Broken with Ithera?"

"Not officially," Nashada said, speaking for the first time, "But I don't think there'll be any question when they discover we've vanished and taken three rikka with us." At Ekkuli's expression, he managed a rueful grin. "We left enough shell to pay for them! But I don't think that will matter much to the House elders."

"Ekkuli," I said. "Come with us. We'll find some het that will welcome us, or start one of our own if need be. Say you will."

The eperu pushed itself to its feet and walked to my rikka. It smoothed its hands over the beast's slender neck and looked up at me, revealing a sudden brass gleam. I saw then what darkness and the curve of its body had hidden from me: my toe-ring, hanging from a leather cord around Ekkuli's neck.

"If you want me, I'll go with you," it said.

"I do," I said, my breath caught in my throat for entirely different reasons. Its mane unveiled was a soft, glowing red-gold not even the starlight could sully.

Ekkuli mounted the rikka we'd brought for it.

"Which way?" Nashada asked.

"South," I said.

"Why that way?"

"Why not?" I said, amused.

Half an hour later, Nashada said, "I suppose we can't have a truedark tale tonight."

I glanced in my pouch. "Not unless Ekkuli knows one that can be performed solely with words composed of the letter *e*."

Ekkuli laughed. "You brought them?"

"Of course. Consider it the beginning of your next collection."

And another hour later, "Ekkuli, you don't mind sharing

Tañel with me, right?"

"I think we could work something out."

"Don't I get any vote in this?"

"Hush, Tañel. You'll get more than enough voting in when you become Head of Household. Let your lovers have their chance."

I laughed.

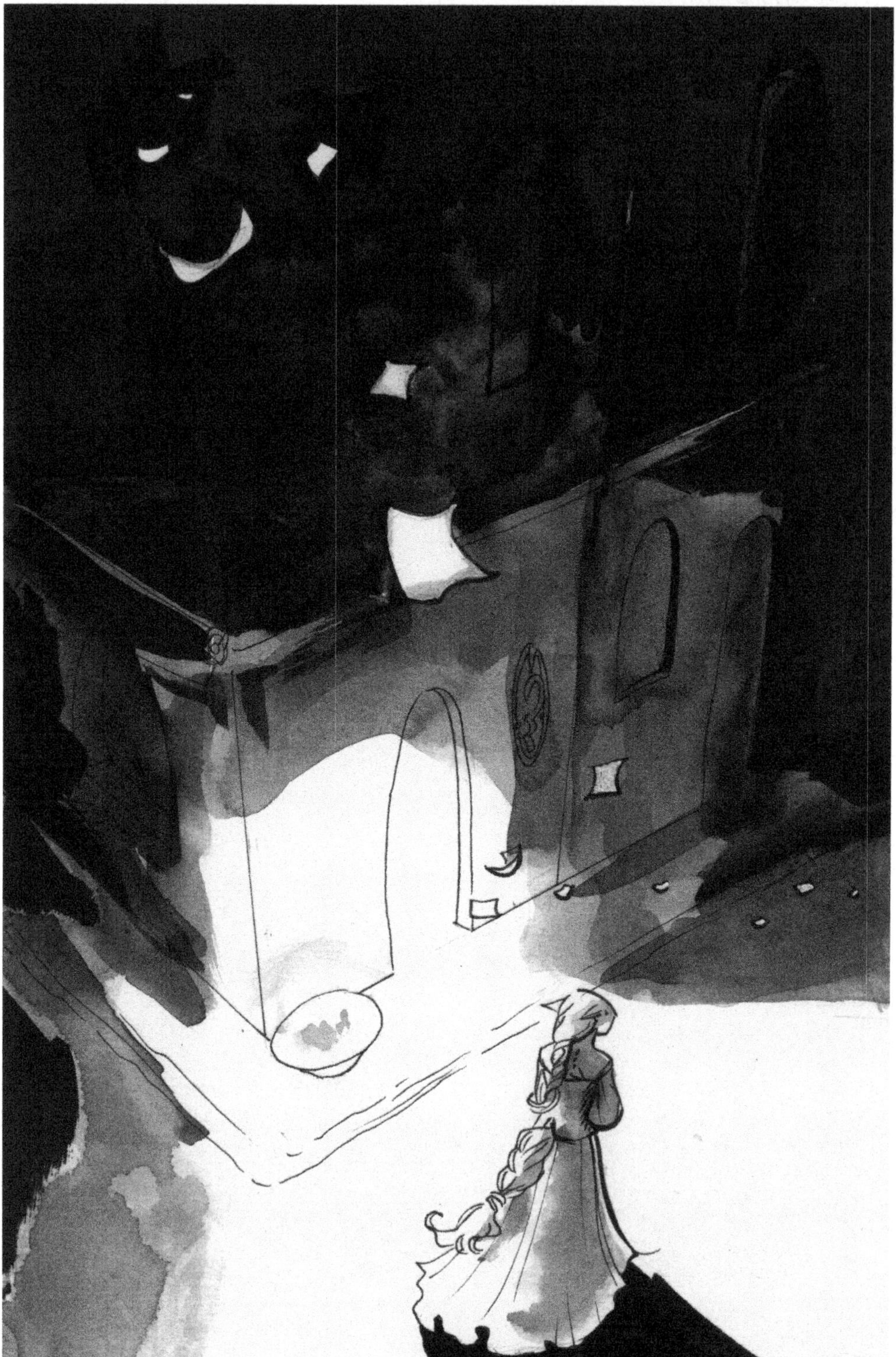

His Neuter Face

*M*Y NAME IS Tafeth Keloi-anadi. This is the story of my change in fortune—a change I had no idea I wanted—and it began with frustration, with my fingers tangled in the laces of my bodice. When the beaded wooden curtain clacked, I glanced over my shoulder, unwilling to turn from the fire and display my clumsiness. Besides, the ability to enjoy warmth without fear was a sweetly valued aspect of becoming neuter.

When I saw my visitor, I did turn, though, tangled fingers and all. "Ke Shuli? I was not expecting you."

Already dressed for the festival, Shuli Waset-eperu, head of House Waset, folded his arms, tail twitching. The firelight glittered on the glass beads woven into his mane and played off the paint on his wedge-shaped head. Tight gray pants ended over the soft curls that spread over his delicate feet-hands—length was in fashion this year—and a shimmering chain of bronze octagons hung from beneath his waist sash, a display of the House's wealth altogether unnecessary given the nature of the festivities.

"Tafeth. I'm sorry to interrupt."

by *M. C. A. Hogarth*

The formality of his voice set my ears back. "How may I help you, ke emodo?"

"I find this difficult to say." He reached down and lifted the stone incense cup from the table beside the portal. His fingers caressed it, and so did his eyes. He wouldn't look at me. "This will be the last festival you celebrate as a part of Waset."

"What?" I whispered, fingers trembling. The loops that trapped them irritated my flesh, and I found it absurd to notice in this moment, when my life was falling to ruin, that my clumsiness was on display. Absurd, and appropriate.

"I'm sorry," he said again.

"But the anadi," I said. "Who will care for them?"

"We will find another," Shuli said. "Please try to understand, Tafeth. If the House is to prosper, we must allow only members of distinction to remain in its ranks. Tomorrow your contract will be offered for bid." He put down the cup. "Enjoy the festival."

I stepped after him, the gown rustling. "Ke Shuli! I was born to this House!"

He glanced over his shoulder. "Yes you were, Tafeth Waset-anadi." And then the curtains parted for him and fell back, beads tangling together.

I sank to the chair beside the fire. In one sentence, Shuli had made his reasons for selling me utterly clear: any Jokkad born female, no matter what sex it Turned at its puberties, was useless to him unless it remained female. An eperu tainted by anadi tendencies would never be as strong as the same neuter had it been born neuter, or even male. Never mind that I was well-suited to my work as guardian to the anadi of Waset . . . I was flawed. The hunting incident had probably only provided a catalyst for the decision.

But for bid! How long had it been since a House had ejected one of its own members in full view of town? Ke Shuli had not even given me the dignity of allowing me to broker my own sale. I had friends in the city . . . had I been allowed, I would have found myself a contract I liked. Now I would have to stand on a dais in front of four handfuls of staring eyes and hope that the highest bidder also offered the best assignment.

I leaned forward, closing my eyes. My cheeks had grown hot, and I touched them with my free hand. As anadi, such heat would have driven me back to the water, or to rest on cool stone and pant. But the eperu I had Turned into was sturdier . . . in body, at least. Still, this sturdiness of body could not hold back the itch of tears at the base of my fangs.

Still trembling, I untangled my hand and resumed threading the laces through the little metal hoops in my bodice. Then I stood and smoothed down the panels of plum-purple and dark brown, the color of stone and soil at twilight. I'd chosen the gown to complement the ginger hue of my skin. Standing in front of the fire, I pulled my glossy hair from the utilitarian braid, arranged my tresses over my bare shoulders.

I hooked the fan to the base of my skirts where I normally would have hung one of the House tokens. Wearing a sign of Waset's prosperity and social influence did not seem appropriate.

In the streets lanterns cast stretched orange circles across the dark blue ground. Streamers of gossamer cloth twirled in the same wind that tousled my hair. I drifted down the thoroughfare toward the Feast of All Beliefs near the center of town. I didn't feel like celebrating, but I had no idea where else to go.

The firelit brick buildings glowed with a sharp clarity in the vespertine dark, as rocks did through a thin stream. I held my arms close to my body, afraid of cutting myself on the world's edges. I felt less than real. All my life I'd been sheltered by House Waset, an older House struggling to renew itself in a climate that favored younger Houses with more shell and fewer choking obligations. I had fought to bring honor and shell to my House, care-taking its anadi, and I was very good at it. When one of the eperu in charge of grading anadi for the town had considered stepping down, I was the one they'd approached to replace it. I had never disgraced our House... until recently.

The center of town had been transformed with pavilions built of stacked brown bricks and expensive, zealously maintained wooden panels. Painted streamers glinted in the falling dark, and the powerful scent of spice cakes and sharp resin incense wafted on the breezes trapped by the collection of booths and wagons.

And there were people... several hundred, all three sexes out in force. The emodo, many of them selling honey candies and tokens from every religion imaginable, seemed to equal in number the eperu, the neuters in their finery. Only the anadi were few, resplendent in their feminine nudity and inevitably escorted by the emodo or eperu of their Houses. A few hours ago, I would have been one of them, also supervising children like the ones who trotted past, their laughter blending with the strains of pipe music and high bells. I did not realize until I stood alone in the crowd how much I had loved my duty. How I should have gracefully declined the invitation to hunt with the other eperu. How costly that hunt would be...

I had never ascribed to any particular faith, and had limited interest in the bewildering array of holy items the vendors lining the square thrust toward me. For lack of any other direction, I approached the central pavilion and sat beside the ramp to dance floor. There I watched the others and let the wind bruise my bare shoulders. I did not allow my eyes to linger long on the eperu shepherding the anadi.

A medallion dropped around my neck, striking the base of my ribcage. I started as a male vaulted onto the ramp beside me and said, "Hail, aspect of the Trifold!"

While I was finding my tongue, the male continued, "As another face of the eternal truth of the Jokku race, I salute you, and embrace you." He paused at my obvious confusion. "And give you a necklace. Are you well, ke eperu?"

My body could not decide whether to stand still or flee, and so I stared at the male. He had a striking face, proud nose sloping to flared nostrils and a grinning mouth with coarse emodo's fangs. The strength and bulk of his body suggested that he'd never been one of the lithe sexes in youth—his wrists alone were twice as broad as mine. His elaborate vest and loin-cloth foiled the plainer pants and blouse, and beneath them his skin shone, a gray shaded blue and black in places. Dark brown hair and brows made his bright eyes astonishing.

I could not pull free of those bright eyes. Could not quite shake from my mind the idea that they were a hunter's eyes, hungry, curious, demanding.

"I . . . I am sorry," I said finally. "You surprised me."

"So I see," he said. He nodded toward the medallion. "Will you accept the gift and embrace me as the emodo aspect of the Trifold?"

"I don't even know what that means," I said, lifting the cool disc and turning it in my hands. My ears, pressed so tightly to my mane, fortunately failed to advertise their blush.

"It means that you acknowledge yourself as part of the truth of our race. Male-female-neuter, we are all yoked. And it means that I have chosen you as my neuter aspect for the night . . . more or less to partner me, while I wander the fair in search of our final face."

My nose wrinkled. "I am no proper eperu. Certainly not enough to serve as your neuter aspect." I tugged the medallion off and pushed the necklace into the male's hand. "Good evening, ke emodo," I said, before walking away.

Footsteps sounded behind my back, and I heard them above all the noise with a clarity that unnerved me. The male was jogging after me. I was considering whether to turn and face him when a strong hand gripped my arm and did it for me. "Not a proper neuter? Ke eperu! You look eperu to me. From your age you're surely past all your Turnings. So why are you no proper eperu?"

I wiggled my arm free. "Leave it be, ke emodo. I am no use to anyone."

"Well, you're of use to me," he said, catching my hand. By the intensity of his voice alone, he halted me and forced me to look into his bright eyes. I flinched from them. "There are plenty of eperu here tonight, ke eperu. I want you for the medallion."

My heart paused. "Why?"

He grinned his hunter's grin. "Because I like the way you look. Good shoulders and hips, a strong face, dream-touched eyes and small hands. Not emodo, not anadi, but yourself, your own creature."

I blushed and looked away.

Once again, the medallion settled over my head and onto my chest. He settled the disc face-upward over my ribs. "Now, will you come with me?"

"What do I have to do, exactly?"

"Just stay near me. Eat with me, if you like. Pretend, for this evening, that we are of the same House, a House of three . . . well, a House of two until we find an anadi."

I swallowed against the itchiness in my fangs so the male couldn't smell any possible hint of tears. "What's your name?" I asked huskily.

"I am just a male tonight. Call me whatever you please, and I shall call you the same." He flashed me a rakish smile and offered his arm. "You do me honor, ke eperu, and the Trifold."

"If you say I do," I muttered, and placed my hand on his arm.

"Better," the male said and drew me into the crowd. The nook I had chosen earlier had secluded me from the bustle of the festival, but I could not avoid the crush on the emodo's arm. Even more Jokka had joined the celebration, thickening the river of people in the streets. I found myself pressing closer to the emodo. He didn't notice that, but he did notice me watching the anadi-guardians. "Your duty?" he asked, thoughtful. "That should make it easier."

"Make what easier?" I asked, ears flattening.

"Finding our female face, of course," the male said.

"How do you propose to find an unallied anadi to serve as your female aspect?" I asked, to get my mind off the crowd, the smell of people, the possibility that I might be worth something after all. "Anadi are never without their House escorts."

The emodo's dark brows lifted. "Is there such a thing as an unallied Jokkad, ke eperu?"

I blushed and looked quickly away.

"Naturally I hadn't expected to find an eperu and anadi without a House to partner me tonight," the male said, watching me with his sharp eyes. "Everyone has a home, which has been part of my problem. But fortunately for me, any Jokkad's contract can be bought for enough shell."

I almost choked, and he pulled me into a corner beside a spiced meat seller's booth. The yellow light cast a stripe along the dusty ground at our feet. "You are unallied, is that it? Not just that, but available."

I opened my mouth, then looked down. When he spoke, his voice was wry, but gentle.

"How much you reveal without speaking, my neuter face." He untangled a lock of my hair with one hand. "Your contract expired? Or something else?"

"My House released me," I said shortly, still refusing to look at him.

"Released you! Why?"

"Because I was born anadi. I did not become eperu until my second Turning, and my House thinks I am flawed because of it." There. I had said it: the shame had come out of my mouth, and tonguing it had made it real. I swallowed against the acrid tear-taste.

He said nothing for so long I glanced up at him. He wore a most peculiar look, an altogether unfathomable one. Shaking himself from his thoughts, he took my hand between his slim fingers. "We are missing our anadi face," he said, "without her we are in imbalance. Come."

Mystified, I followed him back to the dance platform and up the ramp, much to my dismay. He turned to me, taking my free hand, and grinned at my expression. "Don't you dance?"

"I dance," I said, but did not add, 'not well when distracted'. "How will this help us find the final aspect?"

"I trust you," he said; then the music started and I found myself in the arms of another emodo. The stage was crowded with Jokka of every sex and color and size. The first male passed me to the second, and I opened my arms for the first female in the interlocked chain of the form.

As my hands landed on the waist of a stout anadi and saw the long line of anadi waiting to be passed down the chain, I understood how I was to select my choice. If only his words had been as transparent. 'I trust you.' How could he trust me, when he'd only just found me . . . and after my confession, no less?

Still, in the matter of judging anadi I had not yet failed. I always knew when a female needed rest and cool waters, when she was stronger than she seemed, how intelligence could be coaxed to live a little longer in her eyes. The strange emodo had given me something to do that I knew intimately how to do. I would not fail him.

I danced, and into my arms I accepted a seemingly endless string of anadi: slender and firm, husky and broad, ranging from the still sharp-witted to those reduced to gentle beasts. As each female came to me, I searched her eyes for the anadi aspect to complete the male's Trifold.

Near the end, I found her in broad hips and flared shoulders, slender waist and eyes clouded but bright, like opals. She had almost foam-colored skin networked with silvery spirals and dots, her black mane and tail sharp contrast to her body. So startled was I by the revelation of her that I fell out of the chain, breaking the rhythm of the two males passing me on.

"You," I said.

"M-me?" the anadi said. Her uncertain voice had not been often used. I could see the words and mind that had been robbed from her, but the steadiness of the anadi's gaze reassured me. Sometimes females stabilized after a few births, lost no more of their wit to the rigors of labor. I sensed this one was of that stripe.

The strange male startled me, stepping out of the dark to stand at my back. His sweat had a spicy tang that made me lick my lips. "Is this your choice?"

I didn't hesitate. She would not dwindle with time and she had enough spark in her life to be a sweet companion. "This one. This is our anadi."

He smiled solemnly and looped a medallion over the female's neck. She glanced at him, eyes wide.

"Gently, ke anadi," the emodo said. "You are with us for now."

The dancers on the floor weaved the pattern around us as we stood together, three-in-one, in starlight that glistened silver as it enfolded us. There was stillness despite the motion framing us—silence despite the noise. Rightness despite the incongruity.

"You! What are you doing with our anadi?"

I turned, saw two flustered House guardians pushing the dancers away to reach us. When they saw the emodo, the guardians stopped, their jaws working.

The emodo smiled, and there was only a veil over his hunter's grin. "She is of your House, ke Jokka?"

"Yes . . ."

"I'd like to buy her contract."

"She's not for sale!"

"A thousand shell?" the emodo said casually.

I gaped at him. The guardians managed little better.

"Too little? Two thousand, then."

"I . . . she . . . we are not authorized to make such a transaction," one guardian said, its ears twitching.

Unruffled, the emodo waved a hand. "I will be by in the morning, to House . . . ," pausing to glance at their House tokens, "Mena, is that it? To conclude the negotiations. Thank you, ke Jokka." When they didn't move, he added, "I'll return her to you at the end of the festival."

I expected the guardians to object, but somehow I wasn't surprised when they didn't. Looping an arm around both our waists, the male said, "Now, let us see what there is to see and taste what there is to taste, my faces."

"Who are you?" I asked, incredulous.

"Ah, ah, ke eperu. I am Emodo tonight. Just Emodo."

The anadi, watching, said, "Complete."

I shook my swimming head.

The male plied us with the wine of crushed fruits, hot and spiced. He fed us succulent meats flavored with honey and gold pepper. He danced with us, exquisite in his handling—never pushing the anadi too far, never holding back with me. Beneath the orange light of the lanterns, he bought us silvery rings for our arms and necklaces of wooden beads and wrought steel for our throats. Through the crowd he directed us with grace and confidence, never faltering. He was, as he'd claimed to be, the essence of Emodo.

"You made a good choice," he said to me before leaving to return the anadi to her keepers. "Your House a bad one."

I watched until the crowd obscured him and the anadi from sight. No doubt the male would succeed in liberating her from her House whether or not her contract was for sale . . . lucky anadi. Envy tasted even more bitter than tears. I ignored it in favor of the small, tired kernel of happiness. On my last night as a guardian to anadi, I had chosen well for a male. No one would hear about it, but I knew . . . and that was enough.

The following morning I packed my belongings in silence. In anticipation of my contract auction, I had dressed in sensible clothes: trousers and a blouse, a tunic over it cinched with a belt. I'd forgotten to remove the medallion when undressing last night, and on a whim I tucked it beneath my blouse. My life at House Waset, my birth-House, filled only two modest bags. I lifted them onto shoulders that had broadened at my second Turning and walked outside without stopping to wish any of the anadi I had loved farewell. If I vanished without explanation, they would assume the best and soon forget my name. Farewells only confused and upset them, and I would spare them that.

The Transactions office was two streets down from Waset, a short but brisk walk along roads chased by small breezes. Thin pieces of paper clung to the passing wind and the odor of candies and incense hovered near the buildings, teasing me with unwelcome reminders of the festival. The night had hinted that I was not as complete as I'd thought I was, that the relatively cloistered life of the anadi-guardian might not hold as much excitement as I wanted . . . but I could see no way to investigate what that meant. Best to resign myself to the auction and whatever my new life would be than to dream of mysterious emodo and their gifts.

Presently I parted the wooden curtain into the comforting familiarity of the Transactions office. I had often visited to oversee the transfer of contracts that awarded House Waset a new anadi; I had even graded anadi here, using the instruments now racked on the shelf inset into the wall: the knotted measuring cord, the candle and flint, the tablets for figuring . . . and at last, the stamps that graded an anadi from best quality to worst, setting her contract's base price for the duration of her tenure in town.

Ke Shuli, my former Head of House, was already awaiting me with Magat, the emodo who oversaw the office's many duties.

I thought I saw a flicker of sympathy in Magat's eyes, for the male and I had often shared opinions on current events during my visits. But he said nothing as he led me to the back of the office, where an arch opened on the courtyard where contract auctions were held. Without looking at either Shuli or Magat, I sat on the stool in the center of the dais and set my bags down nearby. They were talking, but by now none of what they discussed interested me. All that mattered was living through this humiliation as quickly as possible so I could make peace with whatever master bought my services.

The courtyard's benches slowly filled with Jokka, mostly emodo with a scattering of eperu. I knew most of them by House and reputation, and some more personally; my knack for my work inspired many eperu thrust into the role of anadi-guardian to seek my advice. I never stinted—what purpose would it serve to withhold whatever I'd learned?—and so I was popular among many of the het's eperu. It remained to be seen whether my error would make me less attractive to the heads of household who lined the benches. For a moment's flash, I relived it: the spear in my hand, the breath that eluded my straining lungs, the blurring of the grasses as my feet tripped and the ground met my cheek. Proof that I may wear an eperu's shape, but beneath it my body remained anadi's when pushed: clumsy and short of stamina.

Magat stepped onto the platform, the auction bowl cradled beneath one arm. The benches had filled with guarded but intent faces, and in the laps of those in the front row I could see the auction marks, small chips of clay with painted House symbols.

"We are here to auction Tafeth Waset-anadi's permanent

contract. Pay is re-negotiable each year, one hundred shell fine for break fee. Forty percent of the auction price goes to Waset for commission, five percent to Transactions," Magat said. "Let us begin with fifty shell." He walked the aisles with the bowl extended as he extolled my supposed virtues. My skill with anadi. My long service to Waset, which proved my loyalty. My near ascension to town anadi grader, halted only when the eperu I was to replace decided against retirement. Magat didn't have to tell them why Waset was selling me . . . no doubt word of it had already spread. I watched in glum silence as clay chips began to fill the bowl. Fifty shell for a permanent contract was nothing, but the way bidding was going I might not even garner one hundred. Had I been negotiating my own sale, I would easily have received five hundred or more.

"Seventy-five shell . . . anyone else? Seventy-five—Brightness!"

Magat's exclamation drew me from my melancholy. Someone had deposited, not a token, but real money, a conch shell nearly as large as the bowl itself. It had the glossy finish and unscratched body of a shell that had seen few hands, and it was simply the largest piece of money I'd ever seen . . . and no doubt, the largest these Jokka had either.

"I'd like to buy the eperu," said a confident, casual voice, and I lifted my eyes to the emodo from last night's festival. Today he wore the full regalia of a Head of Household, and hanging above the Trifold medallion was the metal emblem of the newest and most enigmatic House in town. His hunter's eyes met mine, and I knew in a breathless instant I had been wrong to doubt that he'd come for me.

Magat stared at the shell, and then cleared his throat and said with admirable calm, "Ke emodo, I do not have enough shell to exchange this so I can pay Waset its fee."

I glanced at the Jokka on the benches and flattened my ears. Some of the younger emodo looked amused and were already putting away their chips, but the rest glared at the upstart Head of Household with less admirable expressions . . . Avarice. Outrage. Even hatred. The older Houses of the het had, like Waset, kept their reputations but lost much of their livelihoods to the newer, more aggressive Houses, those willing to take a chance on trade outside the town boundaries. I had no doubt they were noting this display of wealth and deciding it had been intended as an insult. I wasn't sure I could disagree with that assessment, and my gut wrenched around a spike of fear, as sharp as the remembered pain of falling in the hunt.

This did not even touch that I couldn't imagine him paying so much for *my* contract. Particularly given my history. Had no one told him? As I watched, the emodo pulled another breathtakingly beautiful shell from his pocket, this one a spiral as long as his hand. With a nonchalance that horrified the spectators, he said to ke Shuli, "Catch!" and tossed it.

Shuli caught it awkwardly, eliciting a spatter of laughs from the onlookers. It was hard to tell if that shell was forty percent of the total, but while I doubted Shuli would argue I found the bright white flush in his ears unsettling.

Magat said, "Very well, then. Does anyone else wish to bid higher?"

A comic silence fell then, as if everyone feared Magat would pick him from the crowd and liberate him of more money than that single shell represented.

"Then we shall record that on this day, Tafeth Waset-anadi's contract was transferred to House Keloi. Thank you all for your interest. Ke Keloi? You're wanted to sign the stone."

Hands clasped easily behind his back, the emodo grinned at me as he walked past, following Magat into the office where he and Shuli would finalize the arrangements. With trembling hands I plucked my bags from the dais and resettled them on my shoulders, and in my nervousness I managed to snag my thumb claw on one of the straps. It was in such state that my new employer found me: in the abandoned courtyard, struggling to pull one of my hands free.

He solved my problem by slipping the bag from my shoulder and setting it on his own. The scent of him, the raw power of his presence, stole my breath for a heart's pause.

Then I licked my lips and said, hushed, "Ke Keloi?"

The Head of House Keloi smiled at me. "So others call me, but I hear it is not unusual for the First Among Eperu to be somewhat less formal with the Head of Household and its anadi kaña. I am Añel. You remember Sunife?"

Belatedly, I registered the figure behind Añel as the anadi I'd chosen at the festival. She stood cheerfully in the sunlight, peering at me with alert and curious eyes. The medallion that hung between her breasts made my hand steal to my own, still hidden beneath my clothes.

"You . . . you are crazy!" I exclaimed. "That shell . . . it's years' worth of money—"

"And you were worth it," Añel said, taking me by the wrist ruff and gently pulling me onto the street.

"Now I know you're crazy," I said, stopping. "Ke Keloi—"

"—Añel," he said.

"No Jokkad is worth a shell that big, no matter how good they are at their work!" I said, plunging forward even as my spirit shriveled. I didn't want to do this, but it had to be said. "You need to get that shell back and use it for House improvements, for land, for . . . for something bigger than a single person!"

Añel's clear eyes never wavered from my face as I spoke, but they darkened. When I finished, he said, "I did use it for something bigger than a single person, Tafeth. I used it to buy completion. To buy harmony among the foremost of House Keloi. I bought partnership. And most importantly, I bought the opportunity to show you that you are worth more to me than the opinions others might have of my wealth. The opinions of anyone, for any reason."

His words fell like stones into the well of my soul. I couldn't even gape, I was so overwhelmed. He knew about my accident—he knew!—and he didn't care!

Añel continued leading me down the street, though how I walked on such watery ankles I couldn't say.

"You are crazy," was all I could whisper.

"Silly eperu," Sunife said.

House Keloi stood on the edge of town, and upon looking at its façade I could discern no unusual feature. It was the inside of the House that dazzled, for it had been built for an unprecedented interaction of the sexes and age groups. I could discern no segregation between types of rooms, nothing that would suggest a nursery, an anadi cavern, eperu quarters. Indeed, each room sported a fireplace and an anadi pool on opposite corners of the room.

Many of these rooms were empty, but the ones that had been furnished astounded me with their wealth. Metal sconces cast fragrant pools of light across the walls. The tables, chairs, even the doors had been crafted of velvety wood. Wooden frames elevated the bedding from the floor, saving the mattresses from infestation . . . had any vermin had the audacity to enter such a mansion. Tapestries woven with unusual designs, scroll paintings depicting winding roads through breeze-ruffled grasses, and painted wooden boards decorated the walls. I stumbled as Añel led me past treasure after treasure. When he finally showed me my room, replete with similar amenities, I blurted, "How can I not have heard of you?"

"I just got here a week past," Añel said. He set my bag on my new bed. "This building used to House a farming family, but they moved on when the harvests failed them, or so I gather from the eperu who sold me the property. It took the caravan I hired about that long to set up what I brought. I set a stone in the House of Transactions to indicate my desire to stay here a while and went looking for members for my new House. I found you." He grinned at me.

"But me . . . my flaws . . . "

"Oh, people have poured them in my ears," Añel said. "You are no hunter of game, I hear. I wasn't seeking one. I was seeking a Jokkad wise in the ways of people, and you proved that to me with Sunife."

"Just like that, you know our mien," I said.

"The Trifold calls like to like," Añel said with a laugh and touched the medallion hidden beneath my blouse. "Didn't you know?"

I rested my hand on his and closed my eyes. It was a struggle to allow myself to relax, to believe that maybe, just maybe, I wasn't doze-dreaming. I was in a rich House with an emodo that inspired me and an anadi I had chosen for the gentle spirit in her eyes. I was wanted. I was *needed*.

I let a long breath out through my nose, then looked at Añel. "Well, if I am to be a third of House Keloi's primes, then I should begin by telling you that with your action today you have, in a single morning's work, earned the enmity of almost every House in the het."

Añel canted his head and waited, so I continued, "Few of them earn as much money in a year as you have just paid for me." I managed a weak laugh. "I'm not even sure where Transactions is going to get the amount of shell it'll need to pay my share of that shell once it's done computing its percentage of the commission! You're going to have to do something and quickly to guard your wealth. I hope you keep it in the middle of the House, where at least people would have to work to get to it. And that it's guarded."

"I don't have any guards," Añel said. He chuckled at my horrified look and continued, "Perhaps you haven't noticed, ke eperu, but you and I and Sunife are the only members of House

Keloi. Still, the wealth isn't stored here, so on that count you can rest easy."

"Not here?" I asked, perplexed.

"Come," he said. "You too, Sunife."

"Where are we going?" I asked.

"You'll see," Añel said with a grin that showed off the gleam of his coarse fangs. "I hope you're in the mood for walking."

"Walking!" I exclaimed, but we'd already reached the door leading out of the House and before I could press him for details other matters stole my breath.

Shuli was not the only House Head standing outside Keloi's door, nor was he the most wealthy or impressive. All of the het's elders awaited us on the road, a showy gathering of emodo in fine clothing with fat purses and obviously displayed House tokens.

"Well, well," Añel said before they, in their immense dignity, could speak. Obviously they'd been expecting to cow him into meek silence. "What is this?" And to ke Shuli, "Was your fee not enough, old man?"

Shuli's ears flattened. Mine did. Everyone's did! I wanted to dart back into the building. What was my new Head of Household thinking to insult this much power?

After glancing at one another, one of the emodo facing us said, "Ke Keloi, you are new here, and perhaps unaware of our customs—"

"—I'll grant you that," Añel said breezily.

The emodo scowled at him and finished, "but we would like you to know that we consider your behavior uncouth."

"Being rich, you mean," Añel said. "I'll keep that in mind.

And now, ke emodo, I have business to do, as I'm sure you do also. Come, Tafeth, Sunife."

He turned his back on them—on all the power of the het!—patently expecting us to do the same. Though the hair along my spine stiffened at the crowd's stares, I padded after my new Head of Household, wondering if his brazen fearlessness would be the end of Keloi. Sunife didn't seem to share my concern, but perhaps that was well. Worry is an eperu's water, an emodo's candy and an anadi's poison.

I caught up with Añel a few lengths down the road, Sunife trotting behind me. A furtive glance over my shoulder confirmed that the knot of emodo remained tied outside our door, staring at us.

"What are you doing?" I hissed. "They'll kill us!"

Añel arched a brow. "You're not serious."

"Well, not literally," I said. "But now they'll unite to block our success at every fork. You've insulted them twice! Don't you care what they think?"

"I don't need to," the emodo said. "Even if they tried to starve me of every business contract I undertook, I will not want for shell. I can go somewhere else." He glanced at me. "Surely you're not frightened of them, Tafeth?"

"Of course I am!" I said, staring at him. "I'm shocked that you're not."

"Ah, well. Soon enough you'll see why the future of Keloi does not depend at all on what the grizzled old men of het Nakali think."

Mystified, I settled into stride beside him, and though I desperately wanted to know more I sensed he would answer no more questions. Sunife slipped her hand in mine and I gave myself up to whatever the gods would bring.

Whatever it was, it was far from town.

The shadows had faded to river pebble-blue when Añel turned us off the dusty road. I helped Sunife through the burnt red grasses up slopes that crumbled into rock and pebble, ignoring the pointed stones that tried to wedge between my toes.

"Añel?" I asked, puzzled.

"We're almost there," he called back.

I continued climbing. At least it would be easy to see anyone following us, if anyone had bothered.

Añel squeezed past two boulders as I watched, wide-eyed, expecting him to scrape his chest. I sent Sunife in before me, so my first view of the mountain meadow was the anadi running across the soft yellow lawn, black tail snapping in the wind behind her. There were two lakes, one fed by a thin trickle of a waterfall and the other without wrinkle. A series of caves with dark openings lined one side of the meadow, and near them trees offered shade.

Añel led me after Sunife, indicating one of the caves once we reached the meadow floor. "Look inside."

So I did. My feet scraped against the hard stone floor, and with my eyes I followed the pale track of the sun's rays the short distance they ventured into the mountain. They traveled far enough to light the treasure trove of shells mounded there. Hundreds of shells the size and quality of the one that had bought my contract outright sat on thousands of tinier shells, their pearly colors gleaming with rainbows of unlimited promise.

I was still gaping at this hoard when a satisfied voice said behind me, "You understand now."

I turned to him as Sunife slipped past me to admire the colors. "How—where—how did you end up with this much money?"

Añel stripped off his vest. "Feel like a swim?"

"What?" I said, staring at him.

His blouse was next. "Just don't let the water get into your mouth!" And then with his laughter trailing he was off running with his loin skirts flapping over his pants. I watched him go, too flabbergasted to respond, and only Sunife tearing past with a delighted crow broke me free. Thinking that the world had upended itself, I followed them both out of the cave and into the waters of the still lake . . . the very salty waters. I was still spitting out my first mouthful when Añel's hand broke the water next to me, holding a glorious ivory cockle-shell sprinkled with brown spots.

"They're all along the bottom," he said. "Hundreds of them. You could fish for days and not dredge them all from the bottom."

I couldn't believe it, so I dove and ran my fingers along the bottom of the lake. My claw-tips caught on dozens of scalloped edges. In wonder I surfaced into a splash directed my way by Sunife, who thought the whole affair an adventure. Perhaps she had the right of it; certainly Añel's lack of concern now made sense. Even if all the Houses of the het blocked his progress, he had more than enough wealth to start again. Maybe things would work out after all.

I splashed Sunife back. We spent an enjoyable few hours there, laughing, playing, floating in water that seemed eager to hold us up to the sun.

✤ ✤

We came home to disaster. In our absence, someone had vandalized the House. The beautiful wooden wall hangings littered the floor in various pieces. The expensive wooden seats no longer had legs to hold anyone up. The delicate paper paintings had been slashed. It was very careful work, for the only things that had been destroyed were items typically unavailable to a new House of limited means.

"It's a message," I said. "An unmistakable one."

Sunife wandered through the broken piles with a forlorn expression. Añel only glanced at me with an unreadable look in his hunter's eyes.

"They want us to act our age," I said, not because I thought he didn't understand, but because I was afraid he wouldn't listen.

"And you think I should," he said.

I sealed my ears against my mane. "I don't know what to think," I said. "I want to work for a prosperous House. I want you to prosper. But this can't be the way to do it."

Añel perched on the one desk they'd left him, a cheap thing of clay and stone. "This may be the wrong het for me."

"This may be the wrong approach," I said. "I don't think any town's going to appreciate a young House with too much money."

"Especially when I flaunt it," Añel said.

"Particularly when you flaunt it," I agreed primly. I got the feeling he wasn't taking this as seriously as he should.

"Are there no people in this het who are tired of working for ancient, close-minded Houses, Tafeth? No one at all?"

I stopped trying to clean the mess and stared at him. His

amusement had fallen from him like a veil, and the intensity of his stare unnerved me. "I . . . I imagine so," I said. No, he had chosen me for some reason, and I should show some mettle. I met his gaze as steadily as I could and said, "Yes, I'm sure of it." And the moment I said it, I was sure of it. I had met more eperu, anadi and emodo in my work than many people imagined. I had friends. They would help me, except—I rolled my lower lip between my teeth and said, "It's just that you keep bruiting your wealth. People don't like that."

"And if I kept it hidden," Añel said. "Don't you think people would find out?"

"Eventually," I said with reluctance.

"And then they would still be envious and angry, wouldn't they? They might start by muttering their poison words amongst their like-minded peers, but eventually words would beget action, and we would be back here," he indicated the broken chair, "wouldn't we."

I sighed and sat on the ground, my shoulders sagging. "What do we do?"

"You do what I saw that you do best, what I chose you as First Among Eperu for," Añel said, and so bright was the fire in his hunter's eyes that the words seemed to burn my ears. "You find me the people who are tired of the old ways. Who want to work hard for better pay. Who want the adventure of a new House, of trade with other het, of a new life. Find me those people, those trustworthy people, Tafeth. I know you can."

I couldn't look away. Even nodding took effort, but I did it. One step at a time.

The next day I decorated myself with all the beads and rings I could find. Sunife helped comb out my tail, and her fingers proved unexpectedly deft at plaiting ribbons into my mane. I dressed in my best clothes, the ones painted with white blossoms lined with silver paint. I applied artful cosmetics, lengthening a few of the spirals on my cheeks into graceful arches and giving them discreet leaves and folded trumpet-flower buds.

Then I covered the whole business with a shawl, to keep idle passersby from identifying me, and went out to find Añel a House.

The most popular cheldzan in the city is in town center, a tea shop that is more famous for its spiced fruit soups than its drinks. Esteemed members of society frequent this place, weaving the webs of connection that make the tea shop a cheldzan as well as a place to eat. At any hour of the day you can find the Heads of Household and their primaries on pillows there, leisurely discussing their plans.

Naturally I did not go there.

Instead, I went to Variket's jewelry shop on the eastern edge of town. This cozy shop, with its front brilliantly lit with sunshine and its back cloaked in warm shadows, sells not just beads and baubles for decoration, but the coveted House tokens, used to honor the most valued members of a House. Eperu wear a single hoop earring; anadi have a thicker navel ring; emodo don the heaviest ring of all, inserted just above the tail where the spine is thin enough to be encircled. Rare is the Head of Household who actually purchases these tokens himself... he sends a trusted eperu to do it for him. In this way, eperu meeting one another at Variket's discovered that they had similar errands and similar gossip.

I don't know who was the first to linger at Variket's instead of buying their rings and immediately leaving, but I do remember when Variket started serving tea to those who remained. That was four years ago, and it's a better brew than the tea shop's.

Today when I entered four eperu were gathered around a table, along with Variket himself. When I pulled my shawl down around my shoulders, a chorus of gasps ran around the chairs.

"Tafeth!" Deñider said, standing. "We heard you'd been herded from town!"

"Certainly not!" I exclaimed. "Though I'm sure that's what less honorable people would like you to believe."

That, of course, was opening enough for them. They made me a space at their table, Variket filled a cup for me, and over the steam I told them what Shuli had done to me, how he had cast me away with so little consideration, not even allowing me to bargain my own contract, how Añel had saved me from ignominy. I did not skimp detail in my description of the shell that bought me, much to the delight of my listeners . . . and while I didn't tell them how much money Añel had, nor where he kept it, I made it clear that he was rich and knew good people when he saw them. By the time I was done with my story, the shadows had had two hours' worth of deepening and my audience had swollen by another three eperu.

"Anyway," I said, draining my third cup of tea, "Ke Añel has asked me to gather a likely group of people for his examination in two days' time, so he can hire them and pay them exorbitantly to build House Keloi. And I'm out looking for people for him."

My audience exchanged glances: nervous tension, I judged. But they asked the questions I wanted asked and not long afterward I was out in the sun's orange light, wondering which of the eperu at the table would show up at the time and place I'd decided. They would make quick work of spreading the news for me. What good is a cheldzan that doesn't lead to a web of people, after all?

When I got home I found all the debris piled in a single room and a meal waiting for me. I stared at it, then peeked through the rooms until I found Añel helping Sunife with her bath.

"You're doing my work!" I exclaimed.

"No, I'm not," he said. "You're supposed to be finding more people for our House. That's your work."

"But . . . bathing . . . cooking . . . " I waved my hands. "You're not supposed to do those things. You're Head of Household!"

Añel sighed and hooked a wet finger in one of my curls, pulling my head down to his level. "Tafeth. There are only three of us. Should I let Sunife's care go undone because you are busy with other equally legitimate tasks?"

"But I'm an anadi-guardian!" I said, ears drooping.

"No, you're House Keloi's pefna-eperu," he said, naming me first among eperu. "That means someone else will have to be the anadi-guardian. Does that bother you?"

"I . . . I don't know," I said. "I hadn't really . . . I mean I suppose I understood, but—"

Añel set the wash cloth aside and turned to face me, dragging one foot heavy with water from the pool. "Sit."

I sat. Sunife watched us both, curious but not upset yet. Her resilience really was remarkable.

"Tafeth," my Head of Household said. "Would you be happier as an anadi-guardian once we find enough eperu to divide the responsibilities of the House?"

"I like being a guardian," I said and even I heard the uncertainty in my voice.

"That's not an answer to what I asked," he said. "Would you prefer to do this work?"

He deserved a thoughtful answer. Instead of saying the first thing that came to my lips, I folded my arms on my knees and rested my chin on them to think.

It wasn't that I didn't know what the pefna did. The pefna managed the eperu of a Household. It chose them for employment and sent them away if they proved unsatisfactory. It arranged their schedules. Supervised their work. It reported on the state of the eperu's work to the Head of Household.

At least, those were the obvious things. From observation I knew there was far more to it than that. The pefna should have poison teeth, for biting the lazy, and a honeyed tongue for comforting the miserable. The pefna needed keen ears to hear the rumors of romance, and keener eyes to discern the effects of such romances on the relationships among the workers. The pefna needed a hard arm to defend the House's eperu from the blows of external criticism and a harder head to withstand the blows of internal critique from the Head.

The pefna was the best the House had to offer. A model

eperu. And I was no model eperu.

"I don't know if I can do what you're asking me to," I said, not looking at him.

"Nonsense," Añel said. "I wouldn't have chosen you if I'd thought you incapable."

My ears drooped. It was hard to argue with one's Head of Household, so I didn't try ... which is why the hand that slipped under my chin, spreading across my jaw, surprised me. I looked into the hunter's eyes and found them soft with pity.

"You honestly believe it, don't you?" Añel said. "You believe that just because you were born anadi and had some freak accident on a hunting excursion that you're somehow less of an eperu."

I swallowed my tears to keep him from seeing them, but his fingers felt my jaw work anyway.

He sighed and stood, stripping off his shirt.

"What are you doing?" I asked, confused. I wiped my mouth. When he didn't answer, but instead pulled at the laces of his pants both Sunife and I became agitated. "Añel?"

He turned suddenly, whisking his tail out of the way, and pushed the top of his pants down. I gasped at the scars that ran across his lower back down to his spine. The beautiful curve that should have lifted his tail from his rump was broken, a mass of scar tissue too knotted for anyone to ever pierce for the cherished emodo ring. "Trifold! Ke emodo, what ... what?"

He looked at the wall, or at the memories he imposed over it. "I was in charge of breeding contracts once. I gave the kaña to a male who destroyed her womb and the rest of her mind. I didn't know he would be cruel and violent ... by the time I came to her it was too late. I fought the male and fell over an urn, and he crushed me onto it. When my Head of Household found out, he decided I was not deserving of the honor that had been bestowed on me. He ripped out my ring... which at that point required very little aid, since the rest of my lower back was a ruin. I was lucky to regain the use of my legs."

"Oh, Añel," I said, hushed. "I had no idea. You don't walk like your tail..."

"Is ripped up at the base?" he said. "I learned how to conceal it. It hurts, though. It always hurts. There and," he tapped his throat, "here too. You think you're the only one who's made mistakes, Tafeth? Be glad that yours affected only you, and not someone in your care."

I flipped my ears back. "My mistakes are not lesser simply because you have done worse," I said, and I had no idea where the words came from, so bitter, so resentful. Sunife whined at the sound of them.

He pulled his pants back up and retied the laces. "Then how fortunate for you to work for a Head of Household for whom you need only sink lower to serve. I would hate for you to have to worry about exceeding your own abilities."

I stared at him, mouth gaping open.

Añel took the wash cloth back up and sat again at the edge of the bath. Without looking at me and with a voice harder than stone, he said, "Go eat."

One did not argue with such a tone. I went back to the fore of the house and sat in front of my unwanted meal. The soup was cold but I drank it anyway, seasoning it with tears. The acrid dinner sat uneasily in my stomach, and I found myself ripping my bread into tiny pieces rather than eating it. With a sigh I pushed the bowl and plate away and let my head rest on my forearm. I should not have made so light of Añel's past difficulties. He was right . . . it was worse to have been responsible for the hurts of an innocent anadi. Merely the idea of such a thing made me shudder with horror.

He had failed others, perhaps, but it was by accident. He could not have known the character of the male he'd selected for his House's anadi. I, on the other hand, had failed everyone by fault of my own, a flaw in my body. I was a cracked pot. Everyone know that pottery, even mended, always leaked.

How could Añel understand? He'd gone from mistakes and pain to become the rich Head of a Household. He'd moved on. I could never move on from the weakness that hid in my limbs and breath, just waiting for others to depend on me so it could destroy their trust.

The row of eperu at the gate was orderly and quiet, with fixed gazes and the air of intent typical of hunters. I studied them from the door into the House with an uncomfortable mix of pleasure and unhappiness. Here was the task Añel had set me to, all unknowing. I knew I could choose anadi; I did not lack confidence in that. But this . . . this was serious.

This was new.

With a deep breath, I strode to the gate and opened it for them. "Come in. Set your tablets on the table and partake of the refreshment until you're called."

They entered then, a good thirty people, more than even I had expected. I saw familiar faces among them, eperu I'd had cause to work with before, some very high indeed in their households. Some say the whispers in a shell are more enticing than those free on the winds . . . I supposed these eperu would agree. As they settled onto nearby benches to quietly converse and share the House's cool mint tea, I settled behind the desk to begin examining the service plates. Each listed the years an eperu had served at each House, the role it had filled, any special accomplishments or talents and the wage it currently earned. I had spent quite a few evenings in the dusty corners of Transactions, looking up legal plates, not just for anadi but also for eperu and emodo when Waset asked me about breeding and care. Without exception, each of these tablets told a fine story, better than average. Choosing would be difficult.

I began the interviews. It did not take long to shed my nervousness. I had done similar deeds with anadi, and having Jokka who could answer my questions without me repeating them in different ways was a nice change. By morning's end I had a fair notion of each candidate's strengths and weaknesses and an unexpected dilemma: there was not a person I wouldn't hire based on their records alone. I watched them as they took their ease in Añel's courtyard; an entire morning of uncertainty and none of them looked tense or nervous. How was I to choose? Añel could afford to hire them all, but we didn't need them all and it wouldn't do to draw so many eperu from their Houses at once. We would be rich enough in work with ten eperu . . . which meant I had to decide.

For the briefest of moments I considered finding Añel and asking his aid, but pride miscarried that thought before it could fully develop. I had chosen Sunife. I would choose our new workers.

Come to that, I'd found Sunife in a dance. Before doubt could cripple me, I called, "Line up, please."

They were puzzled but did as I asked: thirty beautiful neuters, their manes and tails braided with all the wealth they could muster in wooden and metal beads and colorful glass ornaments. Many of them had the prized single ring in one ear. I had rarely seen so much quality in one place.

I stepped up to the first and looked into its eyes and knew, immediately, it would not be the one. The next also fell to my instincts. Down the line I stepped, searching, searching. I found twelve I liked. Somehow I chose between those twelve just with repeated study. It wasn't just their eyes, understand. It was the way they reacted . . . to me, to my study, to each other, to the long wait.

"Thank you," I said to the twenty I turned away. To the ten remaining I said, "Congratulations. If you are pleased with the terms ke Añel offers, you will become part of House Keloi."

I led them to Añel's study and left them there. I should have been worried that he would reject my choices, but I knew he wouldn't. Instead of remaining nearby, I walked through the House's empty halls to its back door. We had a lovely patio overlooking the hills with their thin trees and mauve groundcover. The stone seats were dappled with pale blue shadows, perfect for relaxing. I sat cross-legged on one of them and closed my eyes.

The wind shifted shadows and light across my eyelids in pleasant patterns.

A weight pressed against my knee. I smelled flower-petal water, but felt no need to coddle Sunife. I'd chosen her for her strength of spirit and trusted her respect for the silence. We enjoyed it together, she and I.

The warm scent of spice and musk was Añel's. He sat beside me on the bench, knees touching.

"They'll be here tomorrow," he said.

"All of them?"

"All of them," he said. "You chose well."

I opened my eyes then. He'd dressed for this business and the honey poppies on his vest glittered with the tiny glass beads strung on the embroidery thread. "How do you know?"

"I know because you selected them, and I trust your eye."

I did not answer. I couldn't, torn as I was between pleasure at having done the work and uncertainty over whether I'd earned his praise. Instead I watched the ruffle of the leaves in the patterns cast on my lap. Añel did not interrupt my thoughts.

After a time, I said, "You haven't even told me what we're going to do."

He ran a hand through Sunife's hair. The anadi shifted her cheek from my knee to his and purred. "I have been thinking of breeding anadi."

I swallowed. Sunife looked so content, though. I trusted her, even if I didn't trust myself. With a low voice, I asked, "Do you think we can?"

"I know we can," Añel said. "I ask myself only if I should."

He seemed to take no offense at my question. I wondered how he could seriously consider this course despite having made such a disastrous mistake. Such audacity! "You are braver than I am, ke emodo."

"Añel," he said absently, reminding me. He stroked one of Sunife's locks from her cheek. "And I am not. Today you demonstrated that to me."

"I did?" I said, surprised.

"Oh yes," he said. He laughed, a faint chuff of a sound. "Today you hunted, Tafeth. With the single-minded intensity of an eperu racing through the grass, you found and chose and brought home sustenance for the House."

"I found you ten eperu," I said. "They came here, I read their records, I made a few decisions. That is nothing like a hunt."

"Oh no?" Añel said. "I was watching from a window, Tafeth. You read, you interviewed, you talked. But then . . . " He looked at me, his gaze considering. "Then you hunted. With your eyes. You stood in front of thirty worthy eperu and you wrestled them down with your eyes alone. They might not have fought you with claws or fangs but it was a hunt all the same." Before I could object, he cast his gaze back over the trees, unfocused. "Do not reject the idea without consideration, ke eperu. I have been on a hunt, from beginning to bloody conclusion. You have not. Perhaps in this I have the right of the thing."

That truth I could not deny, and so I thought about it. "It doesn't seem so great a thing," I offered.

"No," he said. "It doesn't. But tell me, why did you choose Sunife?"

Puzzled, I said, "Because she is resilient. There is a light in her yet, and I judge that it won't fade."

"This strength you mean. I don't see it," Añel said. He lifted one of the anadi's arms, turning it as Sunife watched with perked ears. "Her wrists are narrow. She has no muscles. I doubt she could run longer than a few minutes."

"Of course not," I said. "It's the strength of her mind I'm talking about."

"And that's better than the strength of her body?"

"Of course," I said. "A brute anadi might give birth to many children before she dies, but they won't be much good if they don't have a tender spirit and a quickened mind, will... Añel..."

He canted his head. Maybe a smile flickered at his mouth's corners.

"I'm not anadi," I said. "It's different with eperu. Emodo are supposed to be smart. Anadi are special if they're still mindful. But eperu do all the work of the House, the hard work—"

"—and the hard work is always physical, is that it?" he said.

"No, but, I ... the pefna-eperu—"

"—is ultimately the single most important judge of character in the House, yes?" Añel said. "It is supposed to know the mien of every person here."

"But I failed," I said, breathless. "I failed with you, ke emodo. I turned from you when you needed me and I hurt you."

He drew back.

"I did," I said. "You shared something very important with me which I ignored. I was too selfish. I should have realized it was no simple lesson to me, that you needed acceptance and comfort—Añel, ooh!"

He had caught me in his arms and crushed me in them ... truly crushed, for his corded arms were an emodo's in his prime. No emodo had ever hugged me thus, and I was breathless with it. Charmed. I felt safe.

"Oh, Tafeth, my silly choice, my neuter face."

"It's true," I said weakly. "I hurt you."

"Yes. But only you would have noticed why," he said. He drew back, catching my arms in his long hands. "You made a mistake, but you did not compound it." He took a breath. "You do not have to be pefna, Tafeth. If you want, I will give you to the anadi guardianship. But the new eperu come tomorrow and I must know by then what you choose."

I nodded, licked my fangs.

He stood. "Think about the hunt, Tafeth." And then he left.

I remained on the stone bench with Sunife's cheek once again at my knee. The shadow-leaves moved out of my lap and over the bench, lengthening with the failing sun. The world turned a subtle shade of lilac, and the chirp of evening moths replaced the sounds of the day.

Twilight is a trickster's time. Some say that Fate lives in the twilight, waiting to make choices when life is most uncertain, most out-of-focus. Some say the twilight is sacred, the time the Void and the Brightness and the Earth came come together, each sharing influence over the Jokka.

I have never had an opinion about the dusk. The breeze felt comfortable and Sunife seemed indisposed toward moving, so I remained. I kept vigil as the sun withdrew. Even She failed, but She always returned in the morning.

No, that was too easy.

With a sigh, I looked at my hands, the petite hands my birth as an anadi had bequeathed me. I stretched my fingers, remembering the haft of the spear, the way it had fallen when I tripped. Añel had said to remember the hunt, but that was probably not the hunt he'd been thinking of. Or had he? I had chosen Sunife for the resilience she displayed now, but she had been used poorly in the past. So had I. Añel had chosen me for the attributes I had now.

But he had chosen me because I was a better judge of character than he was. Did that make me a poor choice?

I covered my face. I simply couldn't do this. I couldn't decide. I did not have Añel's confidence, nor Sunife's trust in others. I was a crippled eperu who'd been paid too much to do work it could not possibly be qualified for. How could I do what Añel had asked?

The answer was simple.

It had been a long day. I slipped off the bench and held out my hands to Sunife. "Come, let's get you to sleep, ke anadi."

"No."

I blinked. Shaking my head, I said, "It's late, dear one. You need to rest where it's cool and quiet."

"No," Sunife said again.

"You don't want to go in?"

"Can do it myself." Sunife uncoiled.

I smiled. "I know you can. Go, then. I'll join you in a while to see you settled in."

Sunife stopped at the door and said, "Not you."

I frowned at her. "What do you mean?"

"Not you, never," she said firmly. "You are pefna."

"I—Sunife—"

"I am kaña," she said, and I couldn't disagree.

"You are kaña. Most precious of all anadi. Of course, dearest."

"I say you are pefna. Not guardian. Forever," Sunife said and dared me with my eyes to override her.

"You don't understand," I said after a moment's shock.

"No," she said. "I understand. You not." She turned her back on me and entered the purple shadows of the House, leaving me speechless on the patio.

And then, as I stared at the space she was not, I started laughing.

The following morning I presented myself to Añel in his study. I had woken before the sun and attended to myself properly, applying scent to the back of my ears, choosing a vest that accentuated my colors and trousers that were both comfortable and lovely. Most importantly, I braided my hair into twin plaits on either side of my head, tight braids woven with beads and bells. I'd braided my tail as well, one thick rope that held a ringed ornament at its base with a tucked roll.

"Good morning, Tafeth," Añel said. His eyes did not miss the braids, an eperu's braids.

"I have made my decision," I said.

He canted his head.

"Sunife has spoken," I said. "I will be your pefna."

A thin line furrowed his brow. "You cannot allow other people to make your decisions, Tafeth."

"She made *my* decision," I said. "I mean that exactly. I won't regret it, ke emodo . . . and neither will you." I bowed, touching my fingers to my throat and then to my head in an eperu's respesct to an emodo. Then I let him search my eyes, which he did with his hunter's intensity.

He smiled. "Very well, Tafeth. The others should arrive within an hour. Please, get them settled into rooms for me. For now the basic House duties need attendance, so assign them to cooking, cleaning and care of Sunife."

I nodded. "As you will. We'll discuss the House business, yes?"

"Later," he said. He seemed to relax the longer we talked and the more comfortable I seemed. "We can discuss it as a House, I think."

"That will help make our new people feel more involved," I said. "May I suggest we detail the remaining eperu to guarding the House? Posting them at the gate will make an interesting statement to the community."

"A good one?" he said, arching a brow.

"A strong one," I said. "We are nothing if not that, Añel."

"Yes," he said after a moment. "Yes we are."

"A final suggestion," I said.

He canted his head. "Of course?"

"The debris," I said. "From the vandalization? We should burn it."

"Burn it!"

"A bonfire," I said, showing teeth in a grin. "A fine, celebratory, defiant one. The courtyard is large enough."

He stared at me a moment, then a laugh surprised its way out of him. "I didn't imagine you would ever suggest such a thing, Tafeth!"

"Ah, but I knew you would like it," I said. "It's not for me that I suggest it."

"I do like it," he said, still grinning. "We'll do that. Tonight, perhaps, after everyone's settled in. See to it?"

"I shall," I said.

As I left I saw a shadow cross his face, a sort of puzzlement at my transformation. I left him in its company. It would last, that puzzlement, but as I proved my determination to him it would fade. Añel struck me as a pragmatic emodo. One day I would explain the whole thing to him, when the House was on more solid ground and I no longer feared our standing in the het. One day when we had established our trade and filled our rooms with anadi and emodo . . . maybe even after we had children to tend, I would tell him how in choosing Sunife I had made my own choice about being pefna in advance. I could have chosen a weaker anadi, one who needed me. Instead I'd picked Sunife. An ideal anadi face for a man who'd also needed an ideal eperu face.

And that eperu face was me.

Maybe not yet. Maybe I'd have to grow into it. But who is ever ready for what life offers when it comes?

My braids jingled as I walked. I had rooms to make ready and new family to greet.

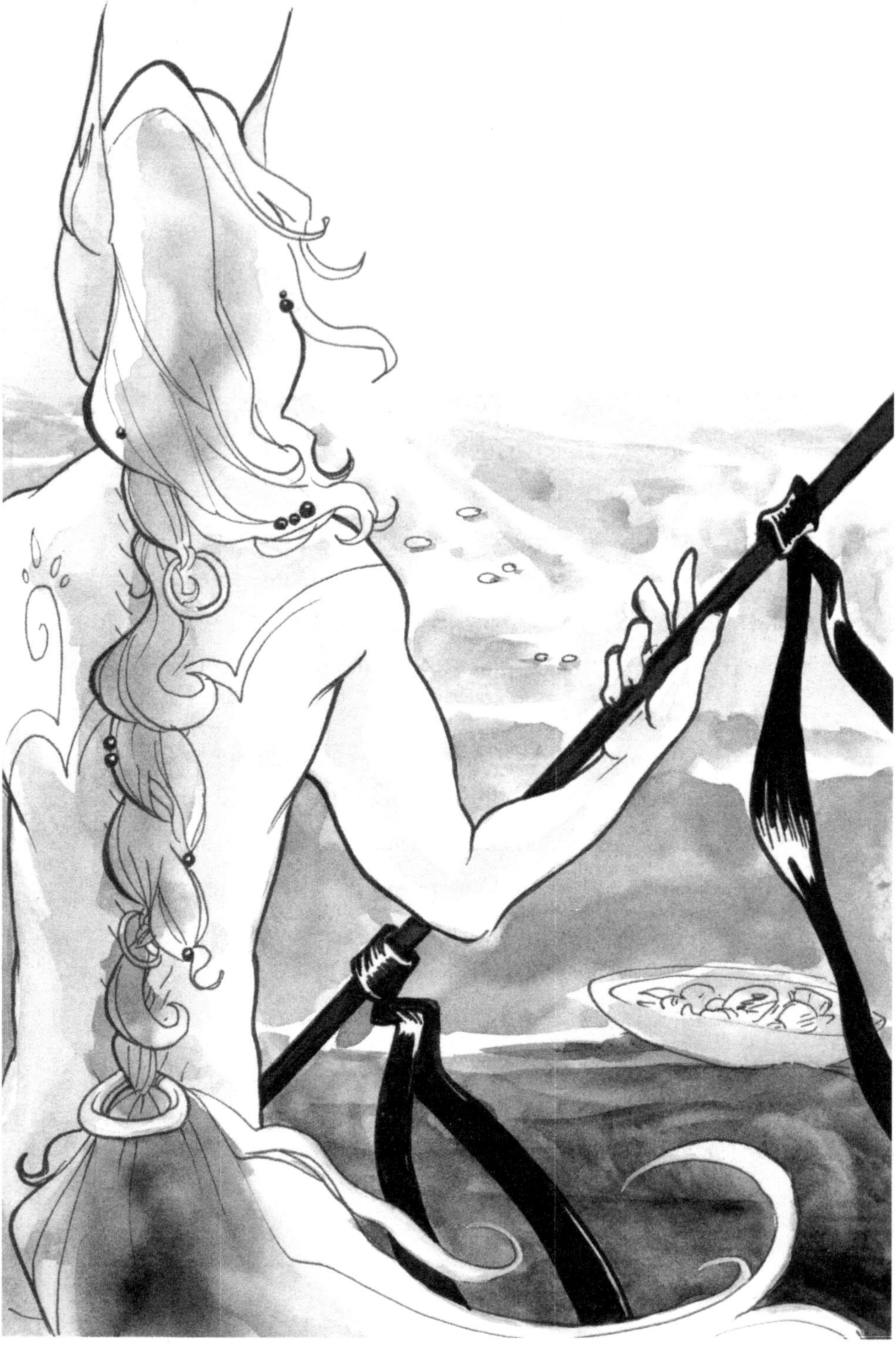

Fire in the Void

"AH... THE BOWL?"

My client's round eyes transfer from me to the offering bowl at the edge of the divining square. His haste in remedying his error amuses me, but most things do. As usual, I keep it hidden behind the mask they expect of the Fire of the Void. I'm not actually a Void-touched diviner, of course, but I must manage a fair deception and an even fairer story, because people always come back.

"What is your name?" I ask my penitent.

"I am Tem—"

"Not your real name," I interrupt. I would get an emodo bent on tripping over his own foot-ruffs for this, my last client of the day.

"Right," the emodo says, eyes growing rounder. I wouldn't have thought it possible. "I am ... the Walker on the Edge of Truedark."

I eye him askance. "That is a perilous name for one seeking the counsel of the Void."

by M.C.A. Hogarth

He shrugs, a nervous flip of his richly-braided tail.

Ah, but what do I know . . . I am only the false seer of House Akkadin. I want only to go home, count my shell and have Bilil wield his steady brush on my heavy hair. "What would you have this Fire cast its light on?"

Now my client shifts from foot to foot, piquing my curiosity. He is a well-formed emodo, I suppose. Neither too stocky nor too lean, with nimble enough hands and feet and a flat nose. His ear tufts are magnificent, but other than that and his elegant clothing I would not have looked at him twice. But what the World does not bestow, visible emotion can grant, and now I find him interesting.

"I said I was the walker on the edge of truedark," he says at last. "I am about to leave the edge and walk into its heart. I would know if this is wise."

I am commonly asked to divine answers to truly stupid questions. My clients would save themselves much time if they would accept a simple response rather than requiring an elaborate ritual that allows them to deceive themselves into thinking this is otherworldly wisdom. "Is this matter relating to business?" I ask. "To the House? To health?"

"To love," he says.

Of course. What else drives us to the most idiotic of acts? I take up my staff, twirling it so that the ribbons float through the air with a soft hiss. Spectacle is important. "I shall draw the question's field, Walker on the Edge of Truedark."

He nods, his cheeks going gray with worry. I ignore him and plant the staff into the soil outside the divining square, then hop lightly into the sand. This is all part of the mystery, the thing I do to convince Jokka to pay me for my common sense. They all think I'm the embodiment of the paradox, the light at night, the star in the smothering firmament. How disappointed they would be to know how it really works. Fire in the Void, my spit.

Still, this part of my work is fun. As the fire bowls flicker near the edges of my square, I dance patterns with my feet-fingers, which are as agile as those on my hands. I swirl the staff around me and the ribbons fray the sand, adding an element of chance to the drawing. Every client gets their own, a diagram I create out of their question and my whim to be the framework for the stones to rest on. For this Walker, my last client, I draw a long wavering diagonal from one corner to the next. On one side I draw our town, het Narel, a few squares here and there to stand in for the Houses. On the other, I add whatever seems aesthetic. A box. A squiggle. A few spirals. The ribbons cut into the sand on the mysterious bank. One of them slashes through a box-house on the town side. I will make good work of that.

When I am done with my dance-drawing, I plant the staff into the soil outside the square and use it to hop back out again. The staff never touches the sand in the square—that's part of the mystery. Handing the bag of stones to the client is also part of the mystery, and my wayward looks appropriately unnerved.

"Grasp a handful of the stones and cast them," I say.

He swallows and does as I ask. The stones flash through the firelight and land with dull thacks on the ground, here, there, everywhere. Six stones, a paltry amount. I set my staff on the cradle carved for that purpose and examine the pattern. The spread reveals the speaker's strength, for they've fallen far from him, but also his nervousness, for they've scattered. This cryptic love affair frightens him, enough that he wants an easy answer to the questions it asks him. An easy answer from an oracle ... the idea is laughable. Doesn't he know my job is to sound portentous and enigmatic? The only easy part of my stories is the end. I always make up happy endings so they'll keep coming back.

So, then. Most of the stones are on the town side of the bank. Only two have fallen on the mystery side. I step into the square to read the symbols I spent several days painting onto my store of stones.

"This affair," I say, keeping a surreptitious eye on his expression, "has disordered your House, for see, here is the symbol of discord and it has landed on this, the symbol of your home."

His ears flatten, but he doesn't contradict me, a good sign. I continue spinning the story. "The discord is not limited to your House. Here I find the sign of the stillness-before-truedark in the corridors between Houses. There is uneasy talk, gossip."

"I thought as much," he murmurs to himself.

"It is costing you money," I improvise, on turning over a stone that landed face-down.

"Yes!" he says.

"—but no one knows it yet," I continue, glad the reversal gives me the opportunity to soften the blows.

"That's luck," he murmurs.

"There is no luck," I say, because it's expected of me. "There is only destiny."

He blushes white.

"Here is love," I say, squinting at the final stone on the town side of the bank. "Your lover lives in another House, but he is half-out of it on his way to join you."

My client shifts slightly. That wasn't quite right, but I'm not sure which part of it didn't work for him. I decide not to elaborate on the possible significance that the Lover's stone had fallen in the house that had been broken by the ribbon's passage, just in case I have the entire thread wrong. "And now we look at the mysterious truedark future. Here is the stone of toil. You will have to work hard on this path you are contemplating."

"No surprise there," he says.

The last stone is hope, which has fallen on the edge of the spiral, like a bit of brush caught in a wind funnel, soon to be sucked out of sight. I like the imagery, but one should always end a reading with a positive image. "And here in the farthest future is Hope, which you will find in a spiral dance of joy."

His ears lift. "Does it really say that?"

"See for yourself," I say, pointing at the spiral. Obediently, my postulant peers at the sign, and his ears and tail perk.

"Now," I say, "reach into the bag for the final stone, the symbol for yourself."

Smiling now, Walker plucks a stone and hands it to me. I turn it over and nearly growl. It's late and I'm tired and I can't figure out how to make a meal of this charred roast.

"What is it?" he asks.

I've hesitated too long in my search for a lie. In a spasm of honesty, I say, "It's the symbol for *nashalan*."

He turns a stunning gray. I wonder if he's going to faint and damage his brain. "That's my symbol? That's me?"

"Yes," I say, and can't blame him for his shock. Had I chosen a stone for a client, it would not have been the symbol for being out-of-place, not quite right, not fitting in. But then, love makes us fools and we often love unwisely, so why not?

"Does this mean my journey is ill-advised?" he asks.

I point at the spiral. "Hope lies at the end of your road, doesn't it? And doesn't a journey often make you grow out of an old shell, until you are no longer quite like the person who existed before?"

This is the kind of talk clients like to hear. The emodo begins to calm. "I . . . I suppose that's so. I may become something new."

"You will find new people to harmonize with," I say, and this earns me a sharp glance. Again I've chosen the wrong thing to say; the self-stone is the last part of the divining and I'm tired. Still, I make an effort to sound all-knowing. "This is the Void's light, thin and clear. Walker on the Edge of Truedark, read what was said by that light and reflect well on it."

"I will," he says. "Thank you."

I nod and turn away until he's gone, then I scoop my stones and the shells back into the pouch—poorly mended, and I'll have to ask Bilil what doze-dreams were distracting him while he plied the needle. What good is an apprentice who can't even sew a proper pouch? Ah, but I am being hard on him simply because it's been a long day. I am full of snarls and swats, but one should not think unkind thoughts about the people who make one's life comfortable. I scuff the sands clean and head home, leaning on my staff. No doubt my clients would be appalled to discover the sacred divining rod of House Akkadin's seer also keeps him from collapsing on the way home... but by my way of thinking, what good's a staff if you can't prop yourself up with it?

"I have a bowl of soup on coals for you," Bilil says.

"I love you," I manage, and he laughs before taking the staff and waving me into the courtyard. As usual, Dekashin is awaiting me, feet resting on a cushion and fingers woven behind its head.

"How was the day?" it asks.

"The day bit my buttocks and spat out the taste of me," I say, and toss it the pouch. I challenge anyone to show me an eperu the match of nimble Dekashin, who one moment is limp as an under-stuffed pillow and the next is snatching a day's worth of money out of mid-air.

"Given how tough and stringy you are, I'm not surprised the day moved on to more tender fare," the eperu says. It glances inside the pouch and whistles. "Well-done! Someone feared the Void today."

"They all fear the Void," I say, shucking my vest and pants. Clad in a long-cloth, I crouch over the fragrant fire Bilil's left smoldering in the center of my courtyard. Ah, but it is good to come home to supper, friends and night-blooming flowers. Taking a deep breath of the perfume, the wind and the rich aroma of the stew gives me enough equanimity to say, "One of these days they'll figure out that I'm making it all up as I go, and that will be the end of this emodo's easy life."

"You call it an easy life and yet I wouldn't trade my work for yours," Dekashin says. "Give me a day of howing and weeding over calming histrionic Jokka too uncertain to make decisions without being told their futures! The rikka are far more tractable."

"You could look at it that way," I say. "But I'd rather dance and make up stories for a living than give myself to the sun's uncertain mercies."

"The sun has not killed me yet," Dekashin says.

I laugh. "Thus speaks the eperu, hardiest of all sexes."

It is now admiring one of the thumb-length shells from my pouch, an alabaster coil of great beauty. "This will please the Head of Household. He's looking to invest in yet another caravan."

"As if the caravans will lead anywhere," I say, tired. "Civilization is burning down. It's just happening too slowly for us to notice."

"Thus speaks the Fire in the Void," Dekashin says, "most pessimistic of all emodo."

I throw a pillow at it and we both laugh.

Bilil appears in the arch with his long-handled brush. "Eat your supper and I'll brush your hair."

"Yes, master," I say, grinning, and reach for the bowl.

Bilil sighs. "You say such things, ke emodo! I am here to learn!"

"You already know more than I do," I say.

"Not true," says my stubborn apprentice. "You may not believe in your own abilities, but I know the Void's voice when I hear it. His whispers saturate you like honey in tea."

I laugh away my unease. "Honey in tea! Even if the Void existed and could speak, I somehow doubt he'd be worthy of such a sweet and homey characterization."

"You may make light of it if you wish, Master. My ears know the truth of it." He sits behind me and begins to ply that brush of his on my tangled mane. My hair sprouts all the way down my spine to my tail, and having someone else to care for it is a blessing I'm genuinely thankful for. Bilil is the richest apprentice in House Akkadin. I would wager he's the richest in het Narel.

"I still laugh to see it," Dekashin says, once again sprawled on its pillows. "If ever I needed proof that there are gods, I have only to see a true believer yoked to a skeptic seer and I know, without a doubt, that our sense of humor is a mimic of a more divine sensibility."

"Ke Keshul believes in his womb," Bilil says with great serenity; I don't have one and never have, but I let him finish his thought anyway. "The belief simply hasn't worked its way up to his head. But it will, eventually. He has the gift, and the gift must come from somewhere." My eyes half-lid with pleasure as the brush pulls at my spine, and I don't have the heart to argue. The Void is nothingness, after all . . . and a gift can't come from Nothing.

I start my duties again the following sundown: more of the usual. People who want to know if they'll Turn, and to what sex. People who are in love and can't figure out why their love isn't returned; or why it's returned when they no longer want it; or why it's not possible because of other duties. Jokka starting new businesses, trying to re-invigorate failing ones, seeking advice on finding new contracts. Jokka concerned with the health and vitality of their Houses. Jokka concerned with their own health and vitality. It is rare for anyone to surprise me with a question.

Still, the predictability means I have a storehouse of patterns I can use in the divining square and as much experience working with that pattern. The less time I spend considering these things, the faster I can move people past the square and the more shell I bring home. My clients are generous as it is—they believe that we donate most of the money to the temple, which we might if I honestly believed I was some kind of seer—so the more of them I work, the better.

Dekashin calls me a pessimist and a skeptic, and I cannot argue that . . . but I love the work. I love dancing by firelight, with the ribbons twirling around my body. I love how the sand's silky warmth drains the longer I work, until at last I know it's time to go home by how cold they are beneath my feet. I love the sound of thrown stones. I love the wonder and interest of my postulants. They're not bad Jokka . . . just misguided. If dressing up my common sense as the Void's wisdom makes it easier to embrace . . . well, who would argue with that?

I am not, however, immune to irritation.

"Walker on the Edge of Truedark," I say, folding my arms over my chest. I hate it when clients come back too quickly—there's a risk of their realizing I'm a fraud if they try to match my divinings too closely to their lives. "You stood beneath the light in the Void just yester-eve. Did you not consider the Void's wisdom?"

"I did," Walker says. He places a shell in the offering bowl, a cowry so large I could probably use it to haul water. Well, that's an exaggeration, but it's at least the length of my palm. "But there are new developments. I need your help, Star of Night."

"Once again this is about love," I guess.

"Yes," Walker says. He trembles where he stands, as if he wants to pace but refuses to move. "But I have a new name tonight. I am Truedark's Raider."

Now the male's pulling names straight out of truedark tales. Maybe he thinks it sounds romantic and portentous, when in fact it makes him sound overwrought. "So you dipped into the well of truedark and came away with a taste of forbidden waters," I say. "Why have you come to me?"

"That taste frightened and also compelled," Raider says. "Both feelings are strong, like rikka yoked in tandem. I can't tell which is stronger."

"Didn't I show you the Hope in the spiral?" I ask, though I have no idea why I'm trying to send him away. He paid—I should deliver. I should be glad to deliver, to addict him to multiple counsels with the Void until he can make no move without paying House Akkadin. Instead, I just want him to go away. Void help me, I have no idea why. I just have a bad feeling about the whole matter.

"That was yesterday, before the rumors in the corridors between Houses came to my ears," he says. "Now things are different. Please, Star of Night, cast for me."

I take up the staff and hop into the square because I cannot look at his worried face and send him away. So instead I dance my drawing, once again adding the diagonal between truedark future and the het. I draw in more squares this time, including the center of town. I add spirals and squiggles and boxes on the opposite side. I do it all without really thinking why, and as I dance the ribbons cut long and ominous wounds in the sand.

I step out and say, "Throw the stones."

Raider digs into the pouch and scatters a handful. More of them, this time. A full twelve. I crouch and begin to search for meaning, and as I do so I struggle with a scowl. Once again, the emodo's managed to find the worst stones of the lot. How do I piece together a story from these dark faces?

"It's not good," he says.

"It is difficult," I say, correcting him. "There is more strife in your House, and here the rumors in the streets have become full speech among everyone in town. There is danger in the het for you and your lover." It sounds like a bad clay drama. Real love affairs rarely have such extreme consequences. I continue, even though I feel as if I'm talking around a swollen throat. "Your business will fail soon, but it seems you have decided against continuing to finance it, which is good, for soon you will have no money. This is a repeated warning—time, haste, all these things appear over and again. Once again, you are called to the other side, the truedark side. A hard work, but I see that someone is going with you. Your lover, perhaps."

"We have crossed over once, but we came back," Raider whispers.

"Remember that Hope was on the truedark's side," I say. "And pick your final stone."

Raider reaches into the pouch and looks into his hand. He wobbles, and the stone falls. As it rolls into the divining square I see that it is once again nashalan. There are fifty stones in that pouch. How he manages to come up with the same one he did last time is a mystery to me.

No, more than a mystery. It's unsettling.

"You must seek your rightful place, Raider," I say. "You are not in it now."

"Yes, Light in the Void. I will consider your words."

"Go," I say.

This time I stare after him as he leaves.

"What happened to you?" Bilil asks at the door.

"I love you," I say, because that part is ritual. And then, because I feel shaken and cold inside and out, I add, "And a pot of hot tea to go with dinner would make me love you more."

"Nothing could make you love me more," Bilil says. "But I will get you the tea."

I stop at the entrance to the empty courtyard. Sometimes Dekashin arrives late; I usually don't notice. Tonight I do. Tonight I have no desire to be alone. Perhaps the tea wasn't worth Bilil's absence. I have never minded silence before.

I wish I had a good story on how I chose this line of work. If I had been given the tale to spin, I might have started, "One day as a child I saw a seer at a festival, and I was drawn to his square..." Or perhaps I'd say, "I once consulted a seer for whimsy and he declared me for the Void..." Or even, "I was passing a temple one day and heard voices whispering to me from inside..." But no, none of those are truth. I came to be an oracle the same way I speak my false prophecies: by making something out of nothing, or at least, very little. I am a story-teller, and people pay more for stories they think are about themselves . . . thus, I learned to be a diviner.

Usually, people ask me harmless questions. They ask me about love and I tell them to give their hearts wholly, or to learn from pain. They ask me about business and I tell them to follow their instincts, and to learn from their mistakes. They ask me about life and I tell them to live it, and to see a pattern in nothingness. Usually if they ask me something that sounds serious or dangerous, I tell them something so nebulous that they'll interpret it to suit themselves.

But this . . . this is different. Every time Truedark's Raider shows up on my square's edge, I feel darkness veiling my sight and I shudder. And instead of telling him common sense, I tell him a hard truth. This is bad for business. It's bad for me. It makes me sound like a real oracle, and no one gives a real oracle money. It's too dangerous.

Bilil crouches across from me with a ceramic pot. Steam wafts from the spout, from the crack lining the lid. "What happened, ke emodo?"

"I wish I could tell you," I say.

"Ah," my apprentice replies, as if I have revealed all. He pours for me, offers me the cup with its bold pollen fragrance.

I eye him. "What do you know that I don't?"

He grins, then shows me the tea-pot. "Here you are, just as it should be, honored Oracle. The vessel does not choose what tea it dispenses. Sometimes it doesn't even realize it's being tipped until the tea pours out."

I scowl. "If you insist on using metaphors, at least use

appropriate ones. Tea is the last thing I'm dispensing."

Bilil sits across from me. "What are you dispensing instead, ke emodo?"

I look into my face reflected in my cup, which trembles, dissolves. "Poison."

I am not at all surprised when Truedark's Raider comes back the following night just as I am preparing to leave—indeed, everything's packed, but I'm sitting there, waiting. He does not come alone.

The veil of the deepest part of night cannot hide this second Jokkad's lissome grace. It is eperu, but it stands too close to Raider for comfort. My comfort.

"Nothing is going right, Light in the Darkness," Raider says. "I have returned to beg for the Void's intercession."

"You must seek that at a temple," I say. "I am no priest."

"You are the Void's voice, His cast light on this benighted world," Raider says.

"Even a voice can do no more than speak," I say, curling my hand so that my palm presses against my fingertips, keeping my claws in. "If you want forgiveness you must go elsewhere. If you want advice, comfort and help, you must go elsewhere. I am only an emodo with a staff and a bag full of painted stones."

"No," Raider says. "You are more. Much more."

I hate him for saying it, but he's not done yet.

"Please, Star in the Firmament. Speak for me and my—"

"—don't!" I nearly cover my face, but I manage to restrain that more obvious sign of my distress. If the emodo is going to be so stupid as to say out loud that this eperu is his lover, I will have no choice but to report them to their House authorities.

But then, perhaps their House authorities already know.

No wonder he flinched every time I referred to his lover as an emodo. To love across sexes is forbidden . . . ah! By the Void if He exists and listens at all! I don't want to be here, with these two very very waywards on my divining square's edge. What if someone finds out they came to me? Together? House Akkadin doesn't need that kind of trouble at its lintel. And I particularly don't need that kind of trouble, and very bad trouble I'll be in if someone realizes I didn't report these two merely on suspicion alone.

Unless I miss the mark that eperu doesn't want to be here at all; good for it. At least one of them has some sense.

"Please," Raider says.

"Truedark's Raider," I say—

"—Running Rikka, now," he says.

Yes, I think. Run far away, Running Rikka. "Running Rikka, the stones have spoken for you already. And they will only work for those who want to hear them." I glance at the eperu.

"I am willing to listen," it says after a moment.

I sigh and pull myself upright. "Think carefully on this—" I pause, waiting for a name. Running nudges the eperu, who says after a moment, "I am the Unnamed."

Perfect. "Very well. Think carefully on this, Unnamed. The light of the Void is cold and thin, like the point of a spear between the ribs."

The eperu shudders. I don't know where these words are

coming from. I don't *want* to know where they're coming from. I almost hate them for being the cause of all this.

"It's not so bad," Running Rikka says. "You just choose stones from this pouch—" He bends, picks it up and the seam Bilil should really have attended to bulges, parts. Three stones fall out. Two roll into the divining square. One lands on Unnamed's foot—a most handsome foot, that, with fingers nearly as impressive as mine. Unnamed must have been an emodo, perhaps even twice. Maybe that's how it and Running Rikka ended up together; perhaps Running refused to relinquish his lover, even when his lover Turned. That, at least, is an old tragedy.

But there are stones on my square. Death is one of them. Grief is the other. And when Unnamed picks up the stone perched on his foot, Running Rikka releases a strangled cry, and I know then that nashalan has reappeared.

"What does it mean?" Unnamed asks.

I look at the stones. "There is nothing left for you here."

Running Rikka trembles, but Unnamed steadies his elbow. The latter leads the former away.

I carefully cart the stones home in their broken pouch. The night seems darker than usual, but there are no clouds, and the staff seems too heavy, a burden rather than an aid. When I appear at the door to Akkadin, Bilil gasps.

"The pouch broke," I say to him.

He ignores the words and pulls me to the courtyard, where Dekashin loses its indolent slouch the moment it sees my face. The two of them hover over me as I fold myself into a knot near the fire, freeing one hand only to scrub at the hair over my nose.

"Keshul?" my best friend asks. I have known Dekashin since we were children together. If it had Turned emodo at one of its two puberties, I think we might have been lovers. Could we have repeated Running Rikka's mistake?

"A bad night," I say after licking my teeth.

"Bad how?" Dekashin asks.

"I . . . I keep forgetting not to say things that are bad for business," I say after a moment, trying to recover my aplomb. "People don't come to me to hear bad news. They don't come to me to hear solutions for true problems. Just for reassurance and positive messages."

"But you have not been able to do that?" Dekashin guesses. Bilil settles onto a mound of pillows, and his body is relaxed and his eyes too knowing.

"I have this particular client who keeps coming back," I say. "And every time he comes back, the stones roll into places that make me feel like . . . oh, it's just ridiculous."

"It's not," Bilil says. "The Void speaks this emodo's future through you, but it's a dark one."

"Dark," I say with a laugh. "How apt."

"Is that true?" Dekashin says. "Are you really speaking his future?"

"Don't be silly," I say, but my voice cracks. Dekashin and Bilil both stare at me. I swallow and say, "Okay. I'm afraid. I'm afraid something's going very wrong with me."

"Sounds like what's going wrong is with this client, Master," Bilil says. "Not everyone's going to have a happy life, especially if they make the wrong choices."

"I don't care about that!" I exclaim. "I care that I seem to be noticing the parts about their not having future happy lives! I'm used to making up the stories, not finding them floating in the Void!"

"What did you truly expect, ke emodo?" Bilil asks. "You are His voice."

I shake my head. "I can't... how could I... how can I accept that? It's silly. It's ridiculous. It's exactly the kind of silly thing I accuse other people of believing. Other Jokka are supposed to be the silly ones."

"So you always say," Dekashin says. "Always asking you common sense questions, paying you for common sense answers. Are you sure it's not the client that's getting to you? Are you sure it's no different from what you usually do? The wisdom of Jokka, you always say, dressed up in the Void's ribbons—"

"This was more than that," I say. "It was beyond that."

"Beyond silly?" Dekashin asks. "What's beyond silly?"

"Stupid?" Bilil offers.

"Disastrous," I say, and feel the hush of the darkness, cold, colder than stars. For the first time, I recognize it.

For the first time, I accept it.

It's bitter as the Void is cold.

Sometimes I wonder if Running Rikka and the Unnamed are dead. I wonder what they took with them. Whether they found water on the unforgiving plains. If they knew to hunt for their food. I imagine them loping along the grasses, hand in hand, trying not to look over their shoulders. I could have told them that the het would send no one after them.

"Will I Turn eperu?"

Naturally, the het gossiped about the sudden departure of Running for several months. Such a mystery! Two Jokka gone without a trace, stealing nothing, not seen. Did they leave during truedark (yes) to have gone unnoticed? And where (south) did they go?

"Should I send my goods on the caravan to het Noidla?"

It didn't take long to redistribute their belongings. Ours is not a rich society. We clothe ourselves in patterned vests and paint designs on our pants, hoping not to notice that we live on the back of the World only by the graces of the gods, who deign to steal our minds only when they do not seek our bodies entire.

"My name is Seeker-of-Wisdom."

"Listen well," I say, holding the staff aloft. "For I am the Fire in the Void, and this is the counsel of the god of night."

I wish I could believe they found Hope in a spiral desert dance.

I know better now.

Chronology

The Age of Mystery

Most history from this time is lost to modern Jokka.

Kediil's Age

The Jokka are migratory nomads. Groups of families are called clans, and wander through set patterns between water-ways.
- "Freedom, Spiced and Drunk"
- "New Stories"
- "A Trifold Spiral Knot"

Ekanoi's Age

The Jokka have settled into rudimentary towns. Sporadic trade springs up between them, brought by caravans led by sturdy *eperu*. Groups of families are far larger and are now called Houses.
- "Money for Sorrow, Made Joy"
- "The Smell of Intelligence"
- "Unspeakable"
- "Unknowable"

Thenet's Age

Trade is trickling to a halt. Towns and cities are frozen at their population levels by lack of resources. In some places, birth rate has fallen below the death rate.

- "His Neuter Face"
- "Fire in the Void"
- *The Worth of a Shell*

Jokku Riha

An abbreviated glossary

aksha [AHK shah] *(noun)*   An expletive. Literally, "entrails".

ana [ah NAH] *(noun)*   night (includes truedark hour)

anadi [ah NAH dee] *(noun)*   female

ba [BAH] *(adjective)*   A prefix used in addressing an individual. Used to address individuals who have not yet reached maturity, roughly maps to "young". Or an adjective version of "child".

cheldzan [chehl DZAHN] *(noun)*   literally "net" or "web"; used for a place where people can gather at any time.

chenji [CHEHN-jee] *(noun)*   Maps closest to "witch", or "shaman" or "magician". In Mysterious times the chenji was an anadi valued for her ability to sense the world's changes and counsel other Jokka on their relationship to the world and one another. Sometimes these anadi were believed prophetic or in possession of magical powers or the favor of the gods. After the Mystery Age, the idea became associated with truedark tales of magical anadi who didn't lose their minds, could curse crops and cast magic and often avenged themselves on others of their race for the injustice done to their sex.

churul [choo ROOL] *(noun)* A gathering to celebrate an initiation, graduation or the completion of another step in a life process (such as final Turning, ascension to certain ranks or professions after study or acclaim, starting of a House, etc.). From the Mysterious Age.

det [DEHT] *(adjective)* Another adjective/title, this one a snide turn on "respected". Used only with contempt.

edloña [eh DLOHN yah] *(adjective)* unspeakable, roughly. Also has connotations of unthinkable and undoable. "Taboo" is also an acceptable translation.

eku [eh KOO] *(noun)* the truedark hour

elithik [eh lihth IHK] *(adjective)* Used to indicate that the Jokkad has been every sex before settling on its final gender. Roughly, "every-sexed".

emodo [eh MOH doh] *(noun)* male

eperu [eh PEH rroo] *(noun)* neuter

het [HEHT] *(noun)* Prefix for a town. Used "het [name of town]".

ide [EE deh] *(noun)* day

isal [ee SAAL] *(noun)*   ocean (much vaster than "the sea").

jarana [jaa RAA naa] *(noun)*   The individual who cares for the anadi of a House, seeing to their health, feeding and bathing those who need aid and arranging for their grading, breeding and care during pregnancy. The jarana sometimes also cares for pre-Turned children, though in larger Houses these duties are sometimes undertaken by separate individuals.

jena [JZAY naa] *(noun)*   heart

jenadha [jeh NAHD hah] *(noun)*   A strategy game played with colored stones, one of the few played by all three sexes.

Jokka [JOHK kah] *(noun)*   Several individuals (plural). One Jokkad, two Jokka.

Jokkad [JOHK kahd] *(noun)*   An individual (singular).

Jokku [JOHK koo] *(adjective)*   Belonging to a Jokkad (possessive).

kaña [KAHN yah] *(noun)*   A title within a House: the most valuable/saleable female therein. The "prize" who will gain the House the most money in contracts. There can only be one of these at a time, though often the title will be traded back and forth as the worth of each female varies.

kaña-befidzu [KAHN yah beh FEED zoo] *(noun)* The most important bred female in the House; a title given to the female whose progeny are considered the most worthy/useful.

ke [KEH] *(adjective)* A prefix used in addressing an individual. Connotes a mild deference, roughly maps to "respected".

kudelith [koo DEH lihth] *(noun)* "three-times-the-same-sexed". A word used for Jokka who have remained the same sex from birth through both puberties.

lithrekid [LIHTH reh kihd] *(noun)* A batlike creature native to southern forests on Ke Bakil, mammalian, with thick, brightly colored wings.

marishet [mah ree SHEHT] *(adjective)* "more of the same". A word used to describe the accentuation of sexual characteristics that occurs when a Jokkad remains the same sex from one puberty to the next.

ñedsu [ne YEHD soo] *(noun)* A hunting beast, slender and about three feet tall at the shoulder with scaled bodies and sleek heads. Hunt in packs.

neked [NEH kehd] *(noun)* forest

oira [OY raa] *(noun)*   A vision or object seen through the stillness of water. Not usually literal, this tends to indicate a truth that cannot usually be seen because it is obscured by movement (like the currents of a stream), but which has been revealed in a second's quiet.

pamari [pah MAH ree] *(adjective)*   kind

pefna [PEHF nah] *(noun)*   A title given to the head of a group within a House. Similar to "master".

relani [re LAH nee] *(noun)*   A gathering for fun; a party. Usually impromptu, but sometimes scheduled.

rikka [RIHK kah] *(noun)*   A beast of burden with slender legs but surprisingly strong. Similar to a large gazelle with a sturdy constitution

setasha [seh TAA shah] *(noun)*   beloved (this word is specific to romantic relationships, and as such rarely is used for people of a gender unlike to the speaker).

sheña [SHEN yah] *(noun)*   The most valued eperu (neuter) member of a Household—the one to whom an earring is awarded. There's only one of these at a time. While the perks vary from Household to Household (and from historical period to period), typically this eperu has more spending money and more bargaining power over its own employment contract.

shekul [sheh KOOL] *(adjective)* A color used almost exclusively for Jokku skin. A gray that is built of a thousand gossamer colors; their sum total seems gray, but to the Jokka's eyes the subordinate colors are also there like faint veils.

sheshil [sheh SHEEL] *(adjective)* A color used almost exclusively for Jokku skin. A dark brown that seems glossy on the surface, but with the suggestion of deeper, hazier browns beneath it.

sukul [soo KOOL] *(adjective)* A color used almost exclusively for Jokku skin. An iridescent blue-white described as looking like a white shell in full moonlight.

Patrons

Thank you to the following individuals who helped make the print edition of *Clays Beneath the Skies* possible with their generous donations:

Bard Bloom
Tiffani Byers
Claire Custer
Lorena Dinger
Bonnie Eisenstadt
Lisa Holsberg
Jari James
Elizabeth Johnson
Amanda Lord
Allison MacAlister
Elizabeth McCoy
Robin Sanford
Toni Sturtevant
Brian and Anna Waite
Denise Walker
Karen West
Leesa Willis
Conrad Wong

About the Author

DAUGHTER OF TWO Cuban political exiles, M.C.A. Hogarth was born a foreigner in the American melting pot and has had a fascination for the gaps in cultures and the bridges that span them ever since. She has been many things—web database architect, product manager, technical writer and massage therapist—but is currently a full-time parent, artist, writer and anthropologist to aliens, both human and otherwise.

Her fiction has variously been recommended for a Nebula, a finalist for the Spectrum, placed on the secondary Tiptree reading list and chosen for two best-of anthologies; her art has appeared in role-playing games, magazines and on book covers.

To keep track of new releases, appearances and signings, visit the author online—

Blog   http://haikujaguar.livejournal.com
Twitter http://www.twitter.com/mcahogarth
Website http://www.stardancer.org

❦ Read More ❦

For the author's available works, a reading order and a buyer's guide, please visit the author's writing page:

http://www.stardancer.org/writing.html

Three sexes.

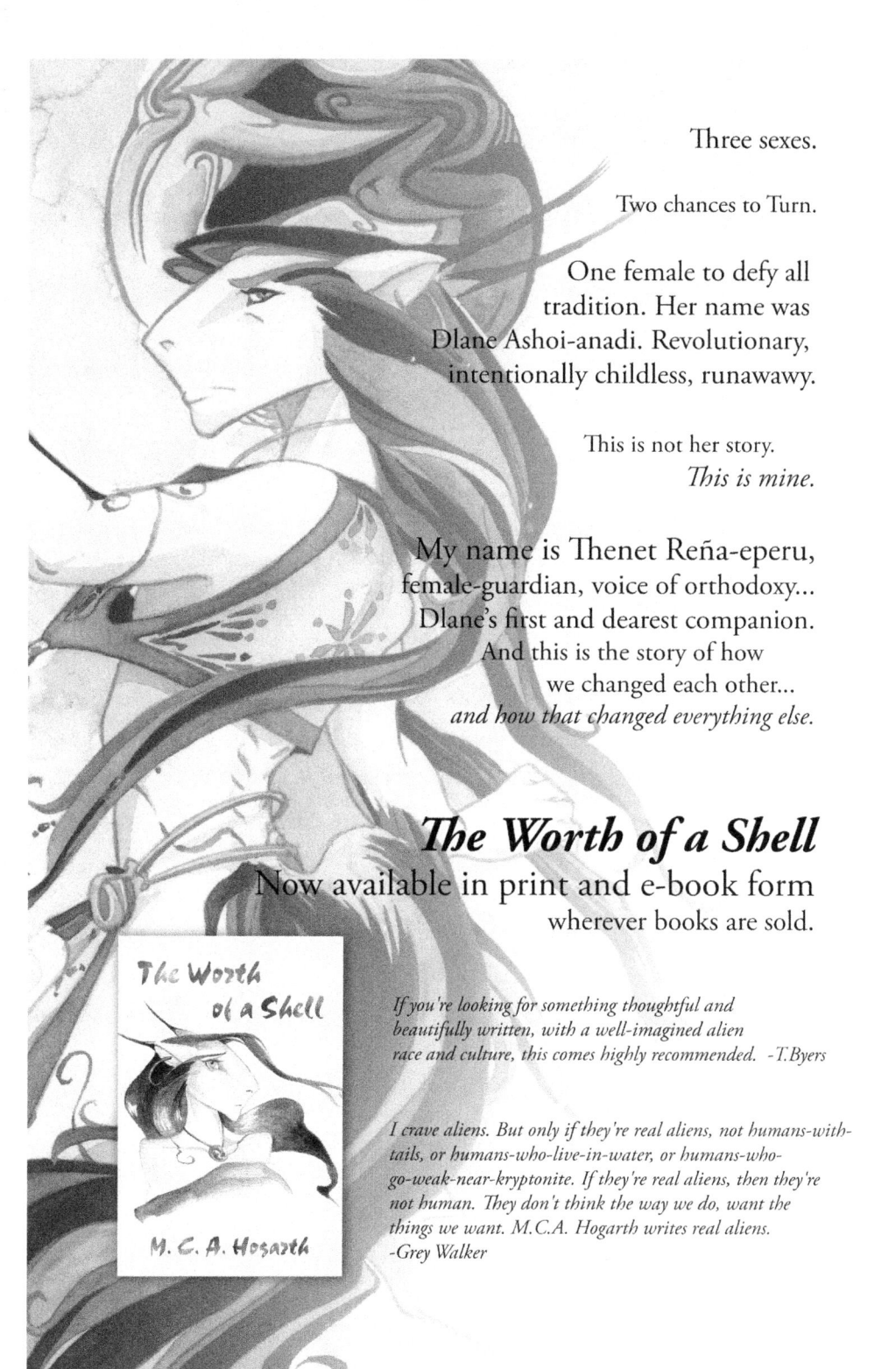

Two chances to Turn.

One female to defy all tradition. Her name was Dlane Ashoi-anadi. Revolutionary, intentionally childless, runawawy.

This is not her story.
This is mine.

My name is Thenet Reña-eperu, female-guardian, voice of orthodoxy... Dlane's first and dearest companion. And this is the story of how we changed each other... and how that changed everything else.

The Worth of a Shell
Now available in print and e-book form
wherever books are sold.

If you're looking for something thoughtful and beautifully written, with a well-imagined alien race and culture, this comes highly recommended. -T.Byers

I crave aliens. But only if they're real aliens, not humans-with-tails, or humans-who-live-in-water, or humans-who-go-weak-near-kryptonite. If they're real aliens, then they're not human. They don't think the way we do, want the things we want. M.C.A. Hogarth writes real aliens.
-Grey Walker

Made in the USA
Las Vegas, NV
03 September 2021